BLOOD MAGIC

ALSO BY T. G. AYER

Young Adult Paranormal

THE VALKYRIE SERIES

Dead Radiance

Dead Radiance Audio

Dead Embers

Dead Embers Audio

Dead Chaos

Dead Chaos Audio

Dead Wrath

Dead Silence

Joshua - Dead Radiance

Joshua II - Dead Embers

Joshua III - Dead Chaos

Joshua IV - Dead Wrath

Joshua V - Dead Silence

THE HAND OF KALI SERIES

Fire & Shadow

Blood & Gold

Time & Fate

Fury & Virtue

Spirit & Soul

THE DARKWORLD ORIGINS

Pyros (Logan)
Ailuros (Kailin)

~

THE DARK SIGHT SERIES

Dark Sight
Cursed Sight
Vissarion
Shadow Sight
Dark Prophecy
Cursed Prophecy
Shadow Prophecy

~

THE APSARA CHRONICLES

Immortal Bound
Gods Ascendent
Dominion Falling
Vengeance Born
Last Legion

~

A SEASON OF ASH AND BONE

Heartfyre

~

Adult Sci-Fi

HANDS ASSASSIN

Death Dealer

Death Mark

Death Strike

Hand's Assassins Series

~

NEW ADULT CONTEMPORARY THRILLER W/A TONI VALLAN

Beautiful Collision

Beautiful Conviction

~

PSYCHOLOGICAL HORROR W/A TONI VALLAN

Dark Shadows

Splinter

Blood Magic
A SoulTracker Novel #1

Cover art by Eduardo Priego
Editor: Tracy Riva
ISBN-10: 0473429241
ISBN-13: 978-0473429249

BLOOD MAGIC

USA TODAY BESTSELLING AUTHOR

T.G. AYER

To Melissa Pearl Guyan
Thank you for sharing this amazing writing journey with me, for
coffees and brainstorming, for shoulders to cry on and kicking butts,
and for generally being one of the most awesome friends I have.
Heart you!

CHAPTER 1

MEL

*H*elplessness is hell. And I knew all about it.

He cleared his throat. "Will you do it, Miss Morgan? The police said they can't do anything more. They have other cases to deal with…more urgent ones." Martin Cross's words barreled out of him in a downpour of hope, and fear that there *was* no hope. A strange combination of emotions I could relate to.

You hope and pray, then you are afraid to hope in case the worst is true.

"Do you have a job?" I asked, my voice absent of emotion.

Cross looked up, startled. He hadn't expected the question. I hadn't yet answered his.

He nodded, the movement a handful of jerks. "I'm a mechanic."

"Go back to work," I said, my tone a little sharper than I'd intended. He seemed about to protest, eyes wide, mouth half open, but I held up a hand. "*If*—and that's an honest 'if'—I bring her home alive, you don't want her to see you falling apart. You need to be strong for her. And I can't promise how long this will take. It may be a week, it may be a few months. I'll find her, alive or not...."

For a moment, confusion darkened his face, twisted his brow. He didn't want to entertain the possibility that his daughter may never come home. And he didn't want to hear me say it. I was supposed to tell him everything would be all fine, that he shouldn't worry and that I'd bring her home healthy and happy.

But I'm not in the business of leading people on. I track, and the results aren't always to my satisfaction. Understandably, people don't like it when their loved ones aren't found or when they turn up dead.

But even dead was something. Dead was closure. Something I'd never gotten.

"You need to be prepared for either result." My words hovered in the air between us as he shifted his gaze away from me.

But Martin Cross had made the effort to find me. That said something. His body said the rest. His haggard face and haunted eyes spoke of fear-filled, sleep-deprived nights, of days where hunger and thirst were the furthest things from his mind. His rumpled jeans and stained shirt, oily unwashed hair that stood in clumped disarray from having those stiff fingers scraped through it every so often—it all spoke of endless days and endless nights of staring off into space, replaying the fateful day over and over, wondering what he could have done differently, going over all his if-only's, falling into bed, unbathed, in yesterday's clothes only to lie there all night, thinking, twisting guilt and hope, grief and anger into an almost tangible knot that lay in his gut, slowly taking him over.

I watched him, hands on the graffitied wooden table, fingers twisted so tight the knuckles gleamed bloodlessly, nails bitten to the quick and jagged at the corners. He unraveled his fingers for a moment to pick up the folder in front of him, turned it around and pushed it toward me. I didn't move.

He'd moved the file only an inch. He didn't think I'd believe him, didn't think I'd take the case. And maybe he was right.

Still, I planned to listen, at least.

I pulled the file toward me and opened it. A worn photograph sat on top of a thick stack of papers. A little girl in blue jeans and blonde pigtails smiled back at me. She was missing two front teeth. I didn't answer him. Couldn't give him hope. Not yet.

Again, I didn't answer his question. I glanced up and met his red-eyed gaze. "Do you have it?"

He nodded, reached into his pocket and handed me a crumpled-up Kleenex. I knew what it was before I unraveled the paper. A tiny little off-white incisor sat within the folds of the white tissue paper. Apparently, the tooth fairy had missed her rounds.

Or maybe the kid had missed the tooth fairy?

I set the Kleenex beside the file and moved the photograph to one side. A copy of the police report lay on top of printouts of emailed correspondence with the detective in charge. If anything, Cross was methodical. The last stack of papers said Cross was also a doer. A plastic sleeve sat thick with Missing Persons fliers.

Samantha Cross. 6 years old. Missing.

I handed the fliers back to him, and he nodded more to himself than to me. When he met my gaze again, I swallowed imperceptibly. His hope was a near visceral thing. And I was wearing the mantle of it on my shoulders, would continue to bear it until I knew what had happened to Samantha.

Now, we sat in a truck stop a few miles outside of Chicago, far enough away from prying eyes. I'd chosen the darkest booth furthest from the window. I preferred to keep to the shadows. No sense in advertising my presence.

When he lifted his gaze to mine, I felt a tug of sympathy. I knew that look, saw it all the time. Almost every time someone comes to me, it's the expression in their eyes that answers my final questions. And now his eyes were filled with terror and hope, desperation and hope. As if he didn't dare consider the possibility I could help because there was always a chance I couldn't. He thought I would fail. I could see it in his bleak expression. The threads were beginning to unravel and very soon he'd lose what little faith he still had left. I wouldn't let that happen. I prayed I wouldn't let that happen.

Missing people can be found. Not all missing people are found.

I'm good, maybe even the best I know of. I find people for a living. My business is dependent on people losing people. The idea doesn't sit so well with me, but it is what it is. Not that I need to find people for a living. I could very well choose to find things. Finding cutting-edge nuclear warheads stolen from the government, locating lists of undercover cops within drug cartels —I can do that. Do the job, find the target, no questions asked. But things hold no interest for me. People do.

I find people. And I don't play to lose.

I lost once. Big time. Too big to forget, too big to close the file. I'm still searching, and someday I will find my sister. Until then, I will find other people's lost people.

"Do you think you can find her?" Cross's voice rasped, and he coughed behind crooked fingers.

What he was really asking was if I'd find her alive. I'm a tracker, not a seer. No amount of wishing on my part would predict or guarantee Samantha being found alive.

I rose, and Cross got to his feet, too. Manners, even in a mechanic, are a good sign. "I'll call you if I find anything. And go back to work," I said, before walking out the door. From the corner of my eye, I saw the nod he gave me. I hadn't answered his question, and he seemed to have accepted my decision not to.

I climbed into my truck, satisfied. He'd go back to work, and he wouldn't call. I hadn't mentioned payment. Cross didn't exactly look like a trust fund baby. I sighed. This one's going to be pro-bono.

Now, all I needed to do was find Samantha Cross.

CHAPTER 2

My phone buzzed and I grabbed it from the seat beside me, while keeping my eyes on the road. I swiped it open, gave it a quick glance and raised my eyebrows in surprise. Martin Cross. Considering he hadn't appeared to me to have exceedingly deep pockets, I'd assumed his case would be one of those out-of-the-goodness-of-my-heart jobs.

But Cross was confirming that my payment had been deposited, and I should see it reflected in the account tomorrow. For once, I was happy to have pegged someone so wrong.

I threw the phone back on the seat and peeked at the rearview mirror. It never hurt to be cautious considering I'd pissed off enough paranormal criminals in my time, but no one was following me.

As I drove to the outskirts of town, I wondered again why I bothered with these visits. I could hear Drake's voice. "Why do you waste your time? The man probably doesn't even know you're there."

Drake Darvon was my best friend and my sparring partner. He was also a gargoyle. Real live blue-blooded in-the-flesh gargoyle. Drake didn't realize I went because I needed to. Because something deep inside me drew me to Samuel.

I pulled up in front of the house, a part of me refusing to enter the grand old home, the other part wanting to rush in there and take Samuel away from it all. To take him away and fix him and make him whole again. It still felt like my fault, even though everyone, including Samuel himself, insisted it wasn't. But if I hadn't been so persistent, if I hadn't wanted to find my sister Arianne so badly and finally bring her body home for some closure, maybe Samuel would still be whole. Maybe he would still be around to guide me.

Not that I needed his training anymore, though. Samuel Fontaine had once been *the* Master Teleporter. There was only one person who exceeded him in his ability to cross the Veils and enter the Other worlds. And that was me. A secret only Samuel and I knew.

Both Omega and Sentinel could never be privy to *that* piece of information. Samuel contracted to both organizations, so he was allowed on occasion to do his own search and rescue jobs. My friend Storm, benevolent caretaker of young people in need that he was, had arranged for Samuel to train me, to help perfect my teleportation, thus putting in motion a friendship of a lifetime.

But Samuel couldn't be hoodwinked. He'd forced me to admit that my front as a simple teleporter was a sham. He'd seen beyond that facade, to my ability to astral-project. Then he'd taken it upon himself to train me.

How to teleport better, faster, smarter.

And how to astral-project with more accuracy, to feel for wards, to move with ease through the ether. And to this day he was the only one who knew exactly how powerful I was. How far I could jump, how strong my self-protection had become, that I'd learned to move through most magical wards.

I rested my head on the steering wheel. *Maybe I should just start the car and go home. Maybe Drake was right and coming here only made things worse for Samuel and for me.* No. I punched the steering wheel, as if it was Drake arguing with me. I'd come this far. And Samuel deserved some company. I got out of the car, controlling the urge to slam the door shut. Fishing in my jacket pocket for my keys, I jogged to the porch, as if by walking any slower I would give myself the chance to change my mind.

Beneath the elegant French columns, with their flaking paint, I hesitated only a moment before I slipped my key into the lock, the rest of the bunch jangling against each other as I moved. I was about to turn it when the giant oak door swung inward so hard I had to let go of my keys or go flying inside with them.

Cassia stared at me, her honey-gold eyes as expressionless as she could make them. "Hello, Melisande."

"Hi, Cass." The skin at her eyes tightened. She hated it when I shortened her name. But it didn't matter. She pretty much hated everything I was and everything I stood for, all on account of the fact I ruined her life. I wasn't in the mood for a stare-down so I tugged my keys from the lock, and took special note of the dark glare Cassia gave them, as if I had no right to have them. I brushed past her and headed for the stairs.

"He's not taking visitors," she said, her voice dripping ice as she pushed her tightly spiraled curls away from her face.

I stopped—my foot on the first stair, my hand on a banister badly in need of staining—and glanced back at her. I smiled sweetly. "Well, good thing I'm not a visitor then, isn't it?" I watched as blood rushed to her dusky cheeks.

Cassia smoothed her skirt down, tamping down her anger with the same action. I really shouldn't bait her. She did take care of Samuel. But I wouldn't care less if she left. I'd just hire someone else to look after him.

I turned my back on her and left her to stew in her fury, taking the threadbare stairs two by two, knowing even Cassia would disapprove. Poor Cassia. Samuel's niece hadn't inherited his teleportation powers; being born normal into an almost entirely magical family was a great burden to bear. The problem with Cassia was that she bore it with vicious anger.

Sighing, I pushed Samuel's door open and walked silently to the table by the window. Today, he sat in his rocking chair beside the open bay windows. White gauze curtains billowed on a soft breeze and he seemed to gaze out at the trees, but I knew he saw nothing of the view. My heart twisted for him.

I drew a rickety chair close and sat beside him. "Hello, Samuel," I said, taking his hand in mine. His skin was paper thin, the fingers bony, muscles weak and wiry. His hand twitched as I held it and I smiled. I knew he knew when I visited.

Samuel Fontaine was not an old man. He was in his late thirties, not the age of a man who should be lingering in a rocking chair. I stared at his once handsome face, high cheekbones now jutting out too far, and gorgeous green eyes now faded to a pale luminous non-color.

But sexy Samuel had been gone a long, long time. Ever since his brain got scrambled doing a jump for me.

What a way to go. My hand tightened on his and I had to force myself to remember his frailty. I began to pull away when his fingers gripped mine with an intensity I hadn't felt in months. My heart stuttered as I stared at him, eyes wide.

"Mel?" his voice rasped, as though he hadn't used it in years.

"Samuel? Yes, it's me." I nodded and smiled, tears threatening to overflow.

He blinked, his expression slightly unfocused. Then he frowned. "Are you eating? You look skinny."

I snorted. "Don't worry about me. It's you we are concerned about. We need you back, Sam-Sam." I leaned close and he placed a palm on my cheek. The curtains billowed into the room, white clouds surrounding us in this impossible dream.

"I know, baby. But I'm not done yet," he said, smiling. "The girl . . . she needs me."

My stomach tightened. "What do you mean?"

A few seconds of silence crawled by as Samuel studied my face with far away pale green eyes. "Patience, Melisande. And don't forget what I taught you," he said softly, his voice fading. "Don't forget . . ."

"Samuel?" I called him, but I knew he was already gone, and my heart ached for him.

"He spoke to you?" Cassia's voice rang out, so harsh and cold it dropped the temperature in the room by a few degrees. Maybe the woman was magical after all.

"Yes," I whispered, still holding on to his hand. He'd spoken. He was still there. And what had he meant? "I'm not done yet?" What did that mean?

"What did he say?" Her question broke through my thoughts, an angry tide breaking onto my happy, grateful shore.

I looked up at Cassia and grinned. "He said I was skinny. And he told me not to forget what he'd taught me." I didn't see any reason to tell her the rest. I suspected she'd overheard the last of Samuel's words so that's just what I gave her.

"What the hell is that supposed to mean?" Cassia snapped, her honey eyes flashing. "He hasn't been lucid for months, and you waltz in and he just talks to you out of the blue and says don't forget what he taught you?" She snorted, hands on her hips, eyes wide. "Who the hell do you think you are? You just come in here whenever you feel like, say whatever you want and then leave him to me? Who do you think looks after him? And he talks to you?" Her laugh was hoarse, underlined by a deep bitterness.

I watched Cassia, her anger an almost palpable thing. She was struggling with her own burdens, but all I wanted to do was to slap her as hard as I could across the face.

"You know what? I'm a bit tired of your whining and moaning. I know you've had it tough, but we all have our own bloody demons to deal with. As far as I'm concerned you can just suck it up." The color drained from her skin and I was certain she wasn't sure whether to be shocked, upset, or angry. "Take Samuel, for instance, he's way worse off than you. Maybe someday we will have him back—from what he said today, I am hoping his condition is temporary and wherever he is he's okay and he will come back. But until then we have to wait. So, quit feeling sorry for yourself. If you feel this is all too much and looking after Samuel is a burden, then by all means leave. I'm sure we can find someone else to take care of him."

I'd never voiced my opinion to Cassia before. I'd always steered clear of her, left her to her anger. Now, in the face of my words and my own fury, she seemed startled, unsure of herself.

"You can't make me leave." She lifted her chin.

Really? After everything I said, *that* was all she got? "I'm not making you leave, Cassia. I'm just saying if you aren't happy taking care of Samuel, we can find someone else." I was careful to use the word *we*. A gentle reminder that my presence here was with the kind permission of Samuel's extended family. Not that I needed their permission, but they had eased Cassia into accepting me in the house and I appreciated that.

Now, I watched Samuel's niece as she considered my words. She didn't respond and for Cassia, being short of words was unusual. Then she turned abruptly on her heel and left the room.

"Well, I suppose I got my answer, then," I said to myself.

Samuel chuckled and when I glanced at him, a little shocked, my heart sank with disappointment at the blank expression in his eyes. Then he tilted his head and stared out the window. Sighing, I got to my feet and kissed his cheek. I walked out of the room and left him there alone again.

As I drove, all I could think about were Samuel's words.

I'm not done yet. The girl . . . she needs me.

CHAPTER 3

SALEEM

*S*aleem shifted in his seat. It felt like he was sitting on a rock rather than the supposedly comfortable seat in Chief Roger Murdoch's office at the Chicago police station. Saleem eyed Pete Fulbright who commandeered the seat beside him, the man's stomach making him look more like a whale every time he breathed.

Saleem didn't like the guy he'd been assigned to. Didn't appreciate his attitude toward his job or toward his investigations. But Saleem was going to give Pete Fulbright the benefit of the doubt.

And Saleem supposed his own presence would do some good in allaying suspicions that Chief Murdoch wasn't taking full responsibility for Fulbright's investigation of a paranormal operative.

Fulbright's sudden aggressive interest in Melisande Morgan had caught the attention of the Supreme High Council, and because of their already established working relationship with the CPD they'd asked Omega—instead of their own investigative unit Sentinel—to look into it.

Omega and Sentinel, both powerful paranormal agencies, were interested in a rash of paranormal disappearances in the last six months, something that seemed to also have caught Fulbright's attention.

"So, I trust you will ensure Saleem here has full access to all our Missing Persons files?" Chief Murdoch said as he rose from his seat.

Fulbright reddened as he stood, his back ramrod straight. "Of course, Chief."

After he stalked out of the office and shut the door with a click, Saleem turned to Murdoch. "I don't need those files, you know." Chances were Omega's files on the disappearances were much more substantial than what Fulbright could come up with.

Murdoch smiled from beneath his mustache. "Of course, I know that. It's just better that Fulbright doesn't." The Chief sat, his massive frame threatening to crush his creaking chair.

"So? What has he been up to?" Saleem looked through the window at the warren of desks. Fulbright stood at one of them, flipping through a stack of files while repeatedly glancing at Murdoch's glassed-in office. Fulbright's stomach rose from mid-chest and hung low on his hips, so low over his waistband the man needed suspenders to hold his pants up. Not that body image bothered the detective at all.

"Investigating all of Mel's cases, but especially focusing on the abductions and deaths involving paranormals. I don't know how, but he's managed to hone in on the paranormal cases too well for my comfort. Ask him yourself. He doesn't mind sharing his suspicions."

Saleem nodded and left the Chief's office, heading to the two desks that sat facing each other. A floor-to-ceiling window looked out onto traffic and block after block of aging high-rises.

He sat, and the sound of the chair brought Fulbright's head swiveling toward Saleem. Fulbright did not expect a conversation with Saleem. In fact, he'd made it clear enough he didn't have much respect for Saleem or his presence. He'd barely glanced at Saleem since he'd arrived.

Saleem knew what that meant. Race always played a big part in heightening emotions. But he didn't care. It was bad enough Saleem's Persian descent was clear in his deep olive skin, dark hair and black eyes. As far as appearances went, Fulbright had Saleem pegged. But imagine if this normal human realized he had a bloody Djinn sitting next to him? A real, honest-to-goodness genie? He'd be off searching for a lamp so fast Saleem would probably choke on the detective's dust.

Silencing a snort, Saleem sneaked a glance at his partner, then shifted in his seat again. Time to find out a little more of what made the whole Fulbright-Morgan relationship tick. "So, what's the deal with you and Mel Morgan anyway?" Saleem asked, pasting on the innocent rookie face he'd practiced with his team-leader, Logan Westin, yesterday.

Fulbright gave Saleem an impatient glare as he stacked his files in a pile and pushed them aside. The detective took a deep breath, grunted. "Just something about her that doesn't add up. Her ability to find people when *we* can't is strangely coincidental. Most of the cases we close out as unsolved end up in her lap. And she solves them. Finds the people, dead or alive."

"And you find that strange how?" The sounds of the office hummed around them. Saleem had his own reasons for being there, for watching Mel Morgan, and the more he knew about her the better.

"Nothing I can put my finger on really. Just strange." Fulbright was being reticent and Saleem understood. Most cops didn't like Omega, or Sentinel.

Saleem stared out the window for a moment, then looked at his new partner. Fulbright shifted and threw Saleem an annoyed glare.

"It's an old case, nine years to be exact. A kid went missing. House trashed. Blood everywhere, parents' throats slit. And this Morgan kid standing there, covered in blood, not saying a word. Then we found there's a kid missing: Morgan's younger sister

Arianne. From the blood and the condition of the house, we knew the chances the girl was alive were slim to none, and Morgan was the main suspect. Case closed." Fulbright shook his head.

"So why keep an eye on her now?" Saleem couldn't keep the criticism from his voice but Fulbright was so wrapped up in his own thoughts that he didn't even seem aware.

"I've been looking at the files. And she's just too good at her job to be...normal."

The hairs on the back of his neck stood on end. "And this friend of hers you are investigating?" Saleem asked, almost afraid of the answer.

"A guy named Samuel Fontaine." He went cold. Samuel, the Master Tracker. So Fulbright was on the paranormal trail after all. Saleem just had to find out how much he knew.

Saleem had heard of Fontaine. Powerful mage trackers were rare. Which is why almost every available paranormal tracker was on both Omega's and Sentinel's contractor lists. Including Melisande Morgan. And Fontaine. Until he'd toasted his gray cells on a jump.

If Morgan's paranormal identity was blown, everyone else would soon follow. Fulbright was more dangerous than he could ever imagine.

Fulbright snorted, reminding Saleem of the detective's unpleasant presence. Saleem didn't want to talk to him anymore so he started up the computer and logged into Omega's server to process his initial report.

CHAPTER 4

MEL

My thoughts were a blur, my mind returning to Samuel. What had he meant? Who was the girl he mentioned? My subconscious knew already where I intended to go, and though my mind replayed Samuel's words over and over again, I drove myself through Chicago's abandoned quarter, heading for Storm's place.

Surely, he would be able to make some kind of sense of what Samuel had said. I parked and headed up the stairs of what used to be an old high-rise apartment building. Storm owned it now and housed a few hundred special kids, gifted kids, paranormals who were lost. I'd been one of those children not so long ago. Would have fallen through the cracks in the human system if Storm hadn't found me. If the system had had its way, I'd have ended up in Juvie with all the hardened human delinquents. That would not have been good for them.

But I'd been lucky. I met Dr. Chloe Murdoch and that got the ball rolling in Storm's direction. The cop in charge had wanted an assessment, had been positive he'd get one back saying I was at least a little disturbed, especially considering they had found me standing in the middle of my bedroom, covered in blood and frozen in place. He'd called in a social worker, Dr. Murdoch, hoping to get a recommendation to have me put in Juvie. Only it didn't work that way. Not for the doctor or Chief Roger Murdoch.

Chloe Murdoch just so happened to be a Sensitive. I'd been supercharged after the murder, so high on adrenaline I couldn't see straight, scared of anything that moved. The experience of witnessing my parents slaughtered had shocked me so badly I'd teleported for the first time, my mind and body lost in the ether. Terrified, I'd struggled to get back despite having no idea how. Panic or adrenaline worked eventually, and I'd returned to my body, back in my room to the bodies of my dead parents.

And to a missing sister.

By the time I'd been taken in to see Dr. Murdoch I'd wet myself, from fear, from waiting too long, who knows. Chloe helped get me cleaned up, got me some fresh clothing and calmed me down just by laying her hands on me. I didn't know it at the time, but Chloe had the ability to take away fear and anxiety just by touch. And she'd chosen the best profession to be in to use such a gift.

I hadn't needed a sedative or anything, just Chloe holding my hand and stroking the back of it, asking me silly questions like what my favorite ice-cream was, and did I like shaved ice or cotton candy. I could hear the cops in the next room—I still had a connection to them, could still smell their scent on me. One of them had grabbed my arm a few times so I had a strong link to his feedback—at the time I'd had no idea what it was called— which tended to pull me toward his thoughts.

Later I would learn that attaching myself to a person's feedback wasn't the easiest thing to do, nor was it easy on the body.

He was fuming, thinking Chloe was full of bullshit and that rubbing the back of my hand ain't gonna get them dick. He needed her to get me into Juvie or at least a psych evaluation center, but the doc wasn't doing what she was supposed to.

He was getting antsy and almost barged into the room when someone stopped him. All I got was him saying "Yes, Chief" and cursing inwardly that *Of course the Chief would agree with whatever his wife said.* Then Chloe distracted me and I was glad because the cop wasn't the nicest of men and when he got angry he said some pretty nasty things.

I pulled my mind from my memories and sighed as I parked and headed inside. Storm kept a ground floor office with an open-door policy for the kids. Being an Immortal, he didn't need to do the kind of outreach work he did, so admiring Storm for his charity work was easy.

Admiring Storm himself was even easier. Easy in the blonde, blue-eyed, Greek deity kind of way that made me pretty certain Storm was a god in disguise and just didn't want to tell us which one. Not that it was weird crushing on a guy who was hundreds of years old.

Today his door was open as usual, and I walked right in, through the empty front room and into the inner office to find the Immortal typing diligently on his laptop.

"Hello, Melisande, is everything alright?" He frowned, studying my face as if he could find the answer on the contours of my bone structure.

I shook my head. "No. I've just come from seeing Samuel and I'm worried." I gave him a quick rundown of what happened at Samuel's but mentioned nothing about the girl. Again, I just felt that bit of information was too unusual, and instinct told me it wasn't something I was meant to go telling all and sundry, even if they happened to be Immortal.

Storm rubbed his jaw, the short bristles making a soft ticking sound. "What could he have meant by 'I'm not done yet'?" he asked, more to himself than anything.

"Do you think he's somewhere on some kind of mission that he hasn't told us about? Something that has to do with astral-projection?" I asked. It sounded like the most plausible option, but then I frowned. "But I didn't even know Samuel could astral-project. Do you know if he could?"

Storm shook his head, his expression shuttered. "No, but physical and mental projection are not that far apart, as far as abilities are concerned. Most high-level jumpers could—in theory—learn to astral-project if they wanted to. The other way around is slightly harder, but not impossible."

"But if he is projecting his mind, then why? And where is he? And is there some way we can help him?" I sat forward on the chair, eager to hear what Storm had to say, yet wondering why he seemed to suddenly close off from me.

"Melisande, Samuel must have a good reason to do what he is doing," said Storm, leaning toward me, his voice lowered. I knew what he was doing. He was trying to calm me down. I didn't need calm. Answers and action. That's what I needed. In fact, I didn't need any of this right now. At this moment I had to get on with finding the Cross girl. Storm continued, oblivious to my internal upheaval. "Wherever he is, he just reassured you he is fine. If he needed your help, he would have told you so. Just leave him to do what he has to."

I sat back heavily, and it was my turn to study Storm's face. "You knew."

He was silent.

"You knew and you didn't say a word?" I got to my feet, furious. "You let me mourn him, thinking it was my fault all these months, that *I* was the reason he was nothing more than just a vegetable?"

Storm still said nothing. Of course, he couldn't deny it, nor would he apologize for it.

My hands were shaking and I tried to still them. I had to get away from him before I said something I would regret. "I'm sorry," I said, wondering why I was the one apologizing. "Is Chloe here?"

"In her office," was all he said, but I barely heard him as I turned and left. I didn't storm out of the room either. No point in being disrespectful. He'd done what he had to do. I just had to suck it up.

How does that feel, Morgan? You can dish it out, can you take it too? I laughed silently. I'd said much the same thing to Cassia not too long ago. Irony sure tasted bitter to me.

I stalked to Chloe Murdoch's office two doors down, knocked lightly on the clear glass of the open door and entered as she glanced up from her laptop. She grinned at me over the top of the black frames of her glasses.

"Hey, Mel. You need me urgently for something?" she asked, a worried frown marring her high forehead. She'd grabbed her auburn curls and twisted them into a loose bun at the nape of her neck. You'd think a bun would make her look her age, but she didn't look anywhere near fifty.

I shook my head and sat on one of the chairs before her desk, my hands still shaking. She'd always been my rock, ever since she'd saved me from Fulbright. And still I felt bad to burden her with my problems.

"No. I came to see Storm."

"But you're upset," she said as she rose and came around the desk to take the chair beside me. "You're shaking. What's the matter?" She asked the question, but I knew she didn't need an answer.

She scooted the chair forward and took my hands in hers, holding them within her soft fingers. Almost immediately, they stopped their quivering, the tension fading from my body as Chloe drew it away. What was wrong with me? I really needed to be stronger than this. Stronger than to allow Storm's deception to upset me.

But I had to be honest with myself. It wasn't that. It was the fact the Samuel was projecting his mind somewhere. Someplace where he remained to protect an unknown girl? Damn Samuel. What was he doing and why had he not told me?

Chloe's warmth and energy calmed me down enough for me to talk to her awhile. I told her about the Cross kid, making her aware she would probably be needed sometime soon. Chloe and I had remained close since she'd saved my ass from Juvie. She'd made sure Storm found me a place at Crawdon High and kept me on the straight and narrow so whenever the cops checked in all they found was a good girl who went to school and never put a foot wrong.

What they didn't know wouldn't hurt them, of course.

OUTSIDE OF SCHOOL, Storm had me trained—weapons, martial arts, anything to help me protect myself. And while he tried to help me be physically safe, I went ahead and practiced with the powers of my mind without him knowing.

I practiced projecting, wandering around the apartments in our building and classrooms at school. Soon I ventured further, out of the city. Then one day I found myself projecting to the Tower of London after looking at a photograph in the newspaper. Scary but interesting.

And decidedly addictive.

I soon grew bored with just astral-projection and decided to try physical jumps again. It terrified me. Which is why I'd been determined to master it.

I never told anyone that every time I teleported I tasted blood when I arrived—the memory of my jump the night my parents were killed still fresh in my mind.

I'd teleported the instant their blood spatter touched my flesh; I still remember the demon's face as he watched me disappear. Red skin, muscle-bound arms, as if he lifted weights. And the most terrifying red eyes I'd ever seen. It took hundreds of jumps before the copper taste stopped making me want to puke out my guts.

"Are you feeling better, honey?" Chloe asked, rising to her feet and giving her knees a little bounce to stretch them out.

I nodded, but I wasn't. Maybe my body felt better, but my mind still felt like crap. But I smiled gratefully at Chloe. "Thank you. I'm not sure what I would have done without you."

Chloe frowned. "Well, Storm shouldn't have upset you like that." She looked back at the doorway as if she meant to go charging and tell Storm off for me.

I touched her hand. "No. It wasn't him."

She studied my face, her eyes narrowed, the crow's feet at the corners of her eyes deepening. She was astute enough to know when someone was lying but I'd learned a few things in my time. I hated to lie to her, but I didn't want her standing up for me to Storm—especially when she had no idea what was going on. What I needed to do now was to get going. To get on with my next case.

At last, she nodded, seeming satisfied.

I pushed to my feet, shoving away my self-pity. "I'm sorry. I really should be going. I just needed to let you know about Samantha. That I might be bringing her in, and it probably won't be through the front door."

"So nothing unusual, right?" She winked, her blue eyes filled with amusement.

"Nope." I shook my head and laughed. "Nothing unusual."

CHAPTER 5

MEL

I left Chloe feeling a little better as I turned onto my street. Smiling to myself, I grabbed Samantha's file from the seat beside me. I hurried from the car, headed to the porch and the door to my parents' two-story Victorian. Through the glass paneling on the door, I could see Drake halfway to the threshold as I opened it. The sight of him made me grin wider.

Broad shoulders, dark skin, chiseled jawline and midnight hair. With those looks, along with all his powers, he'd be just fine on his own, romancing the ladies and slaying bad guys, but he chose to stay with me. Something for which I'd forever be grateful.

Storm had partnered Drake with me when he'd taught me self-defense and the art of sword-fighting. Learning the sword from an Immortal is a unique experience. Sparring with a century-old gargoyle is totally another.

"How did it go?" He meant the meeting with Martin Cross but I knew he could read me well enough to know that more than just the meeting had happened today. His obsidian eyes hardened and he said, "Spill." Then he turned and walked off to the kitchen.

I followed, submitting to his bossiness only because I was

starving and I was so drained I needed to recharge. I slapped the Cross file onto the table as Drake spooned steaming chicken fettuccine into my bowl and I began to eat. It wasn't any particular mealtime right now, being somewhere between lunch and dinner, but I needed food and I'd be gone soon, so now was as good a time as any for a meal.

Drake didn't poke or prod, just waited in silence. Sunlight bathed the kitchen, brightening the already white French country decor. My mother had loved her kitchen and I hadn't changed a thing. Hadn't wanted to.

"This is good," I mumbled around a mouthful creamy pasta goodness. Drake smiled. "Stefano's?" I asked.

"Of course," Drake snapped. "What do I look like? Your fucking personal chef?"

I grinned and he relaxed, folding his great muscle-bound arms at his chest as he leaned against the counter behind him. I reached out with my mind, checking on the magic that protected the house. The magic was strong, the protective bubble solid and impenetrable.

Early on I'd known I could feel magic while in the ether, but thanks to Samuel I'd learned how to test magical wards in the solid world, regardless of what plane I was in. It had saved my life a few times.

Only after I was sure did I begin to speak. "So the Cross case is a go. I leave ASAP." He nodded as if he had expected just that.

"Tell me more."

I cleared my throat. "Samantha Cross, six, missing for almost a year. Father is a single parent. CPD closed the case a long time ago."

"Right. You know what I'm going to say." Even as I nodded, he continued, "You have to be careful, more careful than ever."

"So? What is the underground saying?"

He shrugged. "Nothing definite. Nobody can say for certain if the abductions are linked, but you never know. And your success rate can bring too much attention to you." I knew, but it wasn't as if I was about to give up my job.

The silence went on for a bit too long as I deliberated telling Drake. Then I sighed. "And I visited Samuel on my way back," I said, watching his face tighten. I often wondered if he'd been jealous of my closeness to Samuel all those years ago. It might have explained why he was so uptight about my visits. I sat back and told him what happened. And watched his high cheekbones stand out, more pronounced as the skin on his face went taut with shock.

He took a moment to process it, then asked, "So you think he's somewhere else doing something else right now?"

I nodded, swallowing my frustration and anger even as it came boiling up again. "I have no idea what the hell he's doing, but as soon as this case is over I plan to find out." I let my fork fall into my bowl, staring off into space as Drake took it away. He didn't normally clean up after me, and I suspected he just needed something to do. Samuel had succeeded in shocking him too.

Yeah, Drake, I know the feeling.

"So it's business as usual now?" he asked from the sink.

"Yeah, I even gave Chloe the heads up."

"You need to see Steph?" he asked, coming back to me, wiping his hands on a towel. I shook my head. Martin Cross had said he'd given me all the police files so I wanted to check those first before I bothered my BFF. Stephanie Maxwell wasn't paranormal but she'd grown up on the edge of life like I did. And if Storm had limited his help to only paranormals I would never have met her. Now I relied on her and Drake to be my eyes and ears on all things investigative.

Both Steph and Drake had moved in with me when I finished school and Storm gave me the okay to live on my own. By that time, I'd begun tracking. Small jobs—missing pets, lost keys, stolen cars. Nothing dangerous. Just to make a little money off it for the last two years of school—I was never one to sit on my ass for too long. That was two years ago now, although it seemed more like ten. I felt each year, each month, each day pass by—each day since Ari went missing.

Now my eyes fell on the file at my elbow and I pulled it toward me, setting the Kleenex on the table. I sensed Drake head out of the kitchen to the office. He was back at my elbow seconds later, tipping the contents of the tissue into a clear plastic Ziplock bag. I flipped through the file quickly to get the gist of the case. Time, crime scene, evidence, witnesses. Of the latter two, there were none. Drake worked efficiently too, setting crime scene pictures out on the large square wooden table.

The girl had simply vanished from her bedroom. No sign of entry, forced or otherwise. No sign of struggle, which to me meant she either went willingly or she was drugged, and my money was on the drugs. So we had a smart perp. Most likely a demon, because from my experience most kid abductions were perpetrated by demons—unless it was the parents. Third option, of course, was a serial killer/pedophile perp.

Right now, I needed the rest of the evidence from the crime scene—hair and fiber, none of which Martin Cross had access to. Even if I could request them, it would take far too much time. But a message to Chloe would be sufficient to get it moving along.

I looked up at Drake. "I've got to go back and see Chloe, gimme a sec all right?" He nodded, remaining where he was, studying the photos as if something was about to pop out at him with an answer at any moment.

I closed my eyes and centered myself. The first time I'd astral-projected, it had been a complete accident. Part of me was safe in my bedroom, the other part terrified in Alice's Toyland, where I had meant to get my sister a teddy bear. I'd been scared I was going crazy.

I would have been stuck there, if Ari hadn't come to me and held me tight around the waist.

I don't remember what she said but her words had calmed me enough to get my breathing under control. I found the bear, grabbed hold of it and returned to my room.

Empty-handed.

That day I learned astral-projection involved only the mind, and I couldn't move physical things through the planes. I promised myself then I would learn how to move my body through the planes the way I did my mind.

I was seven.

Now, I projected to Chloe's office, glad she was still there. Then I teleported in and knocked on the open door. Chloe looked up. "Mel?"

I lifted my finger to my lips. I didn't want there to be any connection between Chloe and me where the hair and fiber evidence was concerned. She nodded, and I closed the door as quietly as I could and hurried to her desk. She moved paper and pencil aside for me and I wrote her a note.

Samantha Cross disappearance—hair & fiber results plus any hair samples.

Chloe nodded already picking up the phone and dialing. I waited as she spoke. "Hi, honey. How's it going? You want to meet me for a mocha?"

"Mocha" was code for me wanting some kind of evidence from the Chief's department. They had to meet outside the precinct and Chloe would show him my note. Then he'd get the evidence out, and bring it home, making sure to bring out two other similar files to make it look like he was also doing his own investigations.

She rang off and wrote *8pm* on the piece of paper. Chief Murdoch knew the risks and still stuck his neck out to help me. And the only reason was because I usually found the missing people when the incident was supernaturally related. If I sensed the perp was human, I'd just tell the parents and they'd take the info to the police. I'd also tell the Chief. The parents or spouse think they did something to move the case along, the case gets solved, the missing person is found, and everyone is happy.

The supernatural cases usually don't follow such a publicly successful pattern. The person is returned and Chloe helps to do what she can to transition them from normal and ignorant to paranormally-aware. Aware is one thing; accepting something is entirely different. We usually decide whether we think they can handle the truth or not. Often, the victim is pretty traumatized. Demons and other supernatural beings aren't always nice to their victims. Our easiest way out is hallucinogenic drugs injected by the captors—a story Chloe maintains. They go home to their families with Chloe checking in on them once in a while.

I returned to my body, with Drake still flipping through the file. He glanced over at me. "Done?"

I slumped back into my chair. "Yeah," I said, and it was more a sigh than a word. "I'm going over at eight to pick up the evidence."

"Good." He nodded, then beckoned me. "Look, I found something." He pointed at two of the photos.

I looked really hard but all I saw was a neat child's room, not a toy or piece of clothing out of place, with just an unmade bed to say someone had slept in it. "Sorry, I got nothing."

"That's just it. Everybody but me woulda got nothing." His expression was pleased, as if he was proud of himself but blowing it out of proportion. I looked up at him, frowning and he pointed out two images. "These two. The ones of the window. There's a sigil on the sill but you won't see it. I used my dark sight to check if we missed anything. And there it was."

Gargoyles have a form of magical sight that can detect wards and spells. I possessed something similar but Drake's ability was often more accurate than mine. He'd encouraged me to train the skill but given that I barely had time to wash my hair or go shopping for new clothes, I ended up putting it on my to-do list.

Right at the bottom.

"The sigil again?" I asked, my heart racing. "The same as the last one?" He nodded. "Fuck. This is not what I need to hear."

The last time we'd seen a sigil at a scene was a few weeks ago, on a case involving a young missing boy. We'd never found him.

"So, the perp belongs to the same clan that took your last victim. That's about all we know, Mel." Drake was trying to get me to calm down and he was right. It was just a sigil. A demon's mark. It didn't mean anything more than the abductions could be pointed at a particular demon clan. Or that the demon could be trying to fuck with us, send us on a tangent.

"Right, so if we assume they are collecting, then we need to figure out why. In the meantime, you need to get some rest."

"How much sleep can a girl get with abductions on her mind?"

"Stop making excuses and go get some sleep. You have a few hours before eight so go crash. I'll stop 'em if they try to get in."

"I'm sure you will. Just don't destroy the house while you're at it." I waved at him as I climbed the stairs. Fulbright and his team had barged in on us unannounced once already.

Once had been enough and had put us all on high alert.

CHAPTER 6

J'd learned long ago the art of falling asleep when I needed to. Sometimes a nap here and a snooze there was all I got while on a case, and if I hadn't trained myself to get those much-needed z's I'd be a walking zombie and of no use to anyone, least of all the people I was searching for.

My alarm buzzed at seven and I hopped out of bed, heading for the shower. The blast of hot water on my skin did little to soothe me. It was always like this before a search. Ten minutes later I'd donned jeans and a red peasant top and was at the kitchen table again, staring at the Cross file.

"You going to check for the kid before you go to the Murdochs'?" Drake's voice sounded behind me. He knew me well.

I didn't turn around, just nodded and reached for the small plastic bag. It sat in my palm, looking a bit out of place. The tooth was very white, and tiny, with flecks of red-brown blood left on the root. I stood up, paying little attention to the chair scraping across the floor, focusing on the tooth and the vibrations it set off. I hurried to the sitting room, then made myself comfortable on the overstuffed couch.

I needed to relax for this. It wasn't going to be as easy as jumping to see Chloe. I knew Chloe's signature almost as well as I knew my own, having tracked her countless times in the last nine years.

Tracking a new feedback thread was always an unpredictable experience. Like walking in a jungle in the dark, holding onto a thin cord to guide me. I never knew where I would end up with a new tracking, so it paid to be extra careful.

I rested against the pillows and opened the bag. Just the act of exposing the tooth to the air was enough to start me up. The tooth helped—plenty of feedback from the child, which was a good thing. It meant I'd be able to piggyback on the tangible link between Samantha and what was essentially part of her body.

I tipped the incisor onto the bare skin of my palm and was slammed back into the pillows, as hard as taking a punch to the gut. The link was strong—the regular thud of a heartbeat assured me immediately the girl was alive. I didn't have time to enjoy the relief. The next thing I smelled was blood and I didn't dare to imagine what that meant. All I could sense was a rich odor, a coppery aftertaste. I couldn't be sure the blood belonged to the girl and I couldn't be sure it didn't, so no sense in panicking. Wherever Samantha Cross was right now, she was alive.

But it didn't mean she'd stay that way.

I breathed and attached my mind to the energy resonating from the tooth, then began to feel my way forward, to follow it as gently as I could without breaking it. I'd never broken a feedback thread before and I didn't plan to start now. Inch by inch I moved, testing its strength until I reached the point where the link became intangible. This was where it entered the ether and translated into a jumble of interconnected light, sensory, and electric waves.

Now I could move fast. My mind remained tightly connected to the feedback thread, and I raced along at light speed, reaching the Veil in five seconds flat. I only paused long enough to check that the partition between the worlds was intact and my transition through it wouldn't cause any lasting damage. I moved through the Veil, feeling the pulsing energy of the magic of the wall between the earthly plane and wherever it was I was going. The problem with astral-projection is that often you can't identify where you are going until you get there.

That's why I had no idea I'd arrived in the demonic plane until I was fixed in place. I remained invisible, still holding onto the link to the child. The thread had brought me this far, but it would do nothing to help me save Samantha unless I jumped.

And I couldn't. Not yet.

She sat on a cot bed in the middle of a small room. Rusted metal walls and ceiling closed in on the space, an almost suffocating and definitely threatening cell. Her captors had prepared the space for her. They'd given her a small table, crayons and paper to draw, and a pile of books to read.

Someone had at least cared that she was comfortable. But disappointment twisted in my gut as I took note of the drawings on the stone floor beneath her. The spell protecting Samantha vibrated with power, so strong I could feel it push against me all of ten feet away. A large pentagram patterned the floor, so large it encompassed almost the entire room. The outer circle was the source of the odor of blood I'd smelled on first contact with Samantha. A pentagram drawn in blood was a bad sign. Dark magic. Any hopes I could be wrong were dashed at the items in the center of the circle. More blood, bones, hair, a skull. And a scattering of words written in a language I didn't understand.

I shuddered.

I'd need a powerful mage to help punch a hole in this magic.

Are you here to save me? I almost jumped when the voice resonated within my head. I stared at the girl and was disconcerted to find that though I wasn't really there, she looked at me with the most penetrating blue eyes I'd ever seen. It was almost as if she could see right into my mind.

And then it hit me. Samantha Cross was a paranormal. She had just spoken to me in my head. *How the eff do I answer?* I studied the girl's face again then just nodded.

She giggled, her cheeks going a little pink. *My daddy does that too. When he wants to swear and I'm around.* I smiled and shrugged. Astute kid. But easy to be if you can read minds.

My thoughts whirled. The kid had powers, but what was the extent of them? Could these powers be the reason she was taken?

Okay, so if she could hear my thoughts, maybe I could think my questions to her. *My name is Mel Morgan. I'm here to take you home. Are you all right? Did they hurt you?*

She shrugged and spoke again, her voice resonating in my head, *A little when I first got here. But not anymore. Now they just want me to get inside people's heads for them.*

Is that why they took you?

Yes, they want to train me to work for them. She watched me, her face pale now, her forehead scrunched.

Where are we?

Dastra—the demon plane. She spoke as if demons were a run-of-the-mill occurrence for her. And maybe since they abducted her, they were.

Saman—My thoughts were cut off as the sound of bootsteps came rushing along the passage outside. The sounds grew louder as they encroached on the solid metal door at the other end of the room.

Samantha gasped softly. *Go. Before they get here.* She spoke in my mind again. *They have magic. They might know you are here.*

I hesitated, unwilling to abandon the child. But what choice did I have? Even if the demons couldn't see me, I certainly couldn't take her home until I was able to breach the ward. *Okay, but I will come back.* She nodded and smiled at her hands.

I retreated along the thread just as a group of demons entered the room. I couldn't stay to hear what they wanted, and I just had to hope that she would be ok.

I arrived back in my body, exhausted and a little shocked. Drake stood by the window peering through the part in the curtains and I hid my shaking hands under my thighs.

Drake left the window and walked toward me, a frown creasing his brow. "How are you feeling? Did you find her? Is she alive?"

"Okay, yes, and yes." I sighed, slowly regaining some energy as I brought Drake up to speed.

"So, she's a paranormal. Well whaddya know." Drake stroked his chin and looked at my face. I knew what he was thinking. He was comparing her abduction to all the recent disappearances. I'd just done it myself so I couldn't fault him, but I was on edge.

"Yeah, I thought about that too, but let's not go crazy on the speculation. All we know is she's alive and will probably remain alive as long as she serves her purpose." When Drake raised his eyebrows in question, I said, "Seems they've taken her to use her to read people's minds for them." I sighed, knowing I was being stupid to ignore it. "So, we have to assume they've taken other people too, other paranormals for whatever reason. Means we should keep our eyes open on all new cases. And maybe check on the recent ones, too."

"I'm on it." Drake nodded and we both looked at our watches at the same time. "Time for you to go."

I projected to the Murdoch apartment.

CHAPTER 7

MEL

I entered the kitchen, not too keen on catching the couple in any kind of amorous encounter. I shuddered. Just the thought of it made me start thinking of Chief Murdoch, with all his burly bulk, in a different way.

Okay, thinking clean thoughts, Mel.

The low hum of voices filtered to me from the dining room. Slowly, I shifted my location into the other room and moved to the corner near the kitchen door, remaining in projection state in case they had company, but I was safe.

They were both hunched over a box on the dark oak table, which was currently littered with papers, photographs and files. From the expression on Chloe's face, I could tell she was bursting with questions but couldn't ask a one. When the Chief brought evidence home for me, they never spoke about it and I never spoke while I visited. We had to take precautions in case someone was watching the Chief. And with Omega, one just never knew.

I waited near the door, giving it one light knock. It was the most I was able to do, being non-corporeal. The couple looked up in unison staring in my direction. They couldn't see me, but they knew I was there. And they knew the routine.

Before I began to look at any of the paperwork I had to do a quick recon inside and outside the apartment, just in case. I headed off, checking doors and windows, the patios and their tiny backyard.

Satisfied all was clear, I returned to my body and made the jump straight into the Murdochs' dining room.

Chloe flinched as I arrived beside her, then shook her head and laughed silently at herself. She pointed at the table and I made for the evidence box giving the Chief a grateful wink. They both stood beside me as I went through the box, but not to guard the evidence. I knew they were hoping to see what I would find, that they were as eager as I was to find out where Samantha was.

I was rifling through the paperwork when the Chief pointed out a stack of papers sitting beside the box. The reports I needed. Lists of all substances found at the scene, including a collection of four hair samples. Two identified as Martin Cross and Samantha Cross, and the third confirmed as belonging to Samantha's mother, who had left her husband and child two years before.

I gritted my teeth. What kind of mother do you have to be to leave your baby behind? Did she even know what happened to Samantha? I couldn't dredge up an ounce of pity for a woman who could abandon her own child like that. I took a breath and noted that the fourth sample was "unidentified humanoid" hair. I frowned at the description but reached into the box to pull out the sample envelope.

I laid the unidentified sample on the table, then paused to withdraw a small pair of scissors, tweezers, and a plastic bag from my pocket. I set them beside the envelope. Inside I found a pair of red strands of hair. I picked up my plastic packet and propped it open.

Using the tweezers, I lifted a single strand free from the police sample bag and inserted the top end into my packet. I reached for my scissors then cut a piece of the hair off and let it fall into the plastic, not wanting the sample to come into contact with my skin yet. I returned the rest of the strand to its bag and turned my attention back to my piece of the unidentified hair.

Normally I would project immediately and track the whereabouts of the sample but this time something held me back, a dark, sinister feeling that roiled in my gut. I wouldn't have projected at all if it hadn't been for the Chief.

He stepped closer to me and met my eyes, urged me with a flick of his hand, and I understood his need. He wanted a lead even if he couldn't do anything with it. Knowing something was better than knowing nothing at all.

I glanced between him and Chloe, whose expression mirrored her husband's. I gave in—we all pretty much wanted the same thing. I nodded and held the plastic bag in my hand. Slipping two fingers inside, I gripped the hair between the two digits. The strand vibrated with resonance confirming the potent power of its owner. I followed the feedback slowly, an inch at a time, more careful now because the owner was an unknown entity and because the amount of power I felt made me nervous.

Following the thread, I reached the ether without a problem, then began to move toward the Veil. Once I approached it, I sensed the demonic plane on the other side. Not Dastra—where I'd been before—but someplace else.

An unfamiliar entrance to the Veil wouldn't tell me what's on the other side, making jumping an almost death-defying act. I could, however feel the vibrations of the plane, and recognize parallels. All the demonic planes resonate at a similar level. Not the same, but alike enough for me to recognize them as demonic.

Which made projection the only choice.

Once I transitioned through the Veil, I lost all control. A

powerful force grabbed me, tugging on me and I stiffened with shock. I jerked back instinctively, my heart thudding against my ribs.

That was not supposed to happen.

I was always in control of my projections. I tugged back as hard as I could—but nothing happened. I felt as if I was in a tug-of-war but only I was standing in a field of mud, being dragged across the slippery ground toward a deadly cliff.

An iciness twisted in my gut. If I didn't get out of there immediately I was as good as toast. I listened to my instinct and pulled again, putting every iota of strength into it. The hold on me snapped and I flew backward through the Veil. I skittered along, barely holding on to the thread, flying through the ether. The force threw me right back into the Murdochs' dining room, shaking in confusion, unsteady on my feet.

Chloe and the Chief stood in front of me, eyebrows raised at the state I was in. Chloe put a hand on me but I brushed her off. I needed that adrenaline if I was to get my head around what had just happened. I still held the hair sample in my fingers. I shuddered and dropped it back into the bag, wiping my fingers on the back of my jeans.

I slipped the packet in my pocket and was about to turn to tell the Murdochs I was leaving when the air shimmered before me and a blast of energy sent the three of us flying through the room and plowing into the far wall. Wood splintered and dust rained down on us. After a chorus of grunts and coughs we tried to stand, but when I lifted my eyes to the vortex of liquid air before me, I knew we had to get the fuck out of there.

Right now.

I held out my hands, and each of them took one wordlessly. Then I jumped, and even as we surged through the air all our attention remained focused on what was coming out of the vortex. The last thing we heard was his scream of frustration as we disappeared.

I had learned to cover my jump signature so well that few people could track me. We were safe, but from the expression on the Chief's face he knew what was about to happen.

"I hope you have insurance, Chief."

The Chief nodded, his jaw tight. All Chloe said was, "Oh."

CHAPTER 8

MEL

"What the hell was that?" Chloe asked, her voice breaking the tense silence that hung in my living room like a dense and suffocating fog.

"Something very bad," I said, my tone harsh and slightly afraid.

"Did you see it?" Chloe herself was in shock, and the last thing I intended to do was to touch her. My mind was a jumble as it was and I didn't need her to instinctively try and make me calm and tranquil.

"Yeah. I saw him."

"It's a him? Is he a demon?" Her question ended in a high-pitched lilt.

"Yup, it's a him, and nope, he's not a demon." I shivered a little, still unable to believe what I'd seen.

"Is he going to be looking for us?" asked the Chief, glancing quickly at his wife.

I considered his question for a moment. As possible as it sounded, I didn't think so. "No. He won't waste his time. He used my feedback signature to follow me back to your place. He'll be after me. He can project, which is not good. I just hope he can't jump too." I allowed my senses to reach out around the house and feel the edges of the magical protection sheilding it. *All intact. Good.* "He hasn't breached our protection so that's a plus."

Drake walked into the room and his gaze went from Chloe, to me, to the Chief, and then back to me with raised eyebrows. I dusted myself off and said, "Long story. First you need to help me get the Chief and Chloe to a safe place."

"That's all right, Mel." Chloe waved me away. "Just get us to my office. We'll arrange for transport on our own. Maybe it's best we not be seen together?"

I nodded and got up, walking to them quickly. "I'll take you there now."

Chief Murdoch placed a hand on my arm. "Melisande, if I know you at all, you will be blaming yourself for this and I would prefer you didn't."

"But, your apartment . . ." The reminder of what they were about to lose weighed me down.

He raised his hand to stop me from speaking. "It's just an apartment. We're all safe and that's what matters. It's not your fault." He smiled. "In the line of duty, shit happens."

I snorted, but I relented, preferring to avoid an argument with the Chief. "What are you going to say about the evidence?"

"What I would say about any evidence that burns up in my house. I signed it out, and it was destroyed along with my house. What can I do about a freak accident like that?" The Chief shrugged. "Now, if you could get us to Chloe's office we will go home and discover the destruction of our property."

I nodded and held out my hands to them.

CHAPTER 9

With the Murdochs safely at Chloe's office, I returned home and threw myself onto the couch just as the clock struck nine. Was it really only an hour that had gone by? It felt like days.

"You look like shit," Drake said as he walked into the room with a tall glass of soda. He placed it on the tea tray next to the couch and sat beside me. "You've had a bit of an exciting day."

I glanced at Drake, getting only a very neutral expression. "What's wrong?"

"Nothing's wrong. Why does something have to be wrong?" He looked at me innocently, but innocence and Drake didn't go together.

"Drake. I have enough shit to deal with right now. I do not need you keeping things from me." I turned to face the large gargoyle. "So start talking or I will have to make you." I choked down a smile. Here I was, threatening a paranormal with the ability to crush me with his bare hands.

Brazen.

Drake turned and headed out the door. "Fine. You don't have to get all violent on me. Follow me if you want the information straight from the horse's mouth." I hurried out of the sitting room after him. Drake took the stairs two by two, but I followed at a more sedate pace. I knew where he was going. Stephanie Maxwell was our resident computer geek, and her computers lived upstairs in the attic, well-hidden just in case the cops decided to raid my home.

At the top of the stairs, we turned right and climbed a too-narrow staircase that led straight up into the dusty, cobweb-ridden attic. I could feel the hum of the computers from the bottom of the stairwell, something no normal human could do. We'd managed to soundproof the room but couldn't do much about the energy the machines gave off. At least I didn't have to worry about Fulbright's guys hearing it. A paranormal might be able to sense the waves of energy coming from the room. But I wasn't worried about Omega or Sentinel. Both organizations hired me from time to time; both knew what I did for a living. Unlike Fulbright.

Inside the small attic, we maneuvered past the old dusty trunks and boxes piled high at the eaves. At the far end, an old grandfather clock stood beside a warped, gilt-edged mirror that leaned against the wall, providing horribly distorted reflections of those who passed. Drake walked to the clock, and slid his hand behind the ancient piece, pressing the little button we'd installed there. The mirror swung forward on silent and invisible hinges, and we entered the tiny room behind it.

Steph looked up at me, her expression worried, which made me worry.

"What's up, geek?" I asked as I sat on the edge of her desk, but she didn't smile.

"You're not going to like this, Mel." She shook her blonde head as she tapped away at her keyboard, her ponytail swinging as she looked from one screen to another in front of her. Then she pointed at a monitor and I swiveled to have a look.

Six photographs filled the fifty-inch screen, one of them

belonging to Samantha Cross. As I studied them, Steph tapped the enter button and another page of six photos came up. She tapped again and again; a few images were familiar—cases I'd tracked and found the people, some cases where I hadn't been able to bring home a living soul. At last, she came to a screen that held a sickeningly familiar image.

Arianne. My sister.

"Whose files are these?" I asked, my voice tight. I hadn't missed the fact that all the images had file numbers and further details available by clicking on the file. "Did you hack into the CPD's files?"

"Nope. This is Omega's."

"What? Steph, are you insane?" I shuddered to think of what would happen to Steph, to all of us, should she be discovered.

"Nope. This is where the trail led me." She shrugged, clearly not in the least concerned with being found. "Don't worry, they can't trace me. I'm piggybacking on one of the staff who's online right now. As soon as they log off, I'll hunt down someone else who's online. Only problem with this type of hacking is it's limited to having someone working online within their system. As soon as everyone logs off we can't see anything."

I was still in shock she managed to find a way into Omega's files. I cleared my throat. "Okay, so can you explain what led to you hacking Omega?"

"Well, Drake wanted to look at the most recent files on missing persons and I pulled them. Only problem was there seemed to be more than we suspected. And many of the files had the Omega stamp on them. Seems a lot of the missing persons cases were handed over to Omega to investigate."

"Probably looking for a paranormal aspect," I said, almost to myself, not taking my eyes off the screens.

"That's what I thought, so I decided what the heck. It was a good a time as any to hack Omega. So I did. And this is what I found. All CPD's missing persons cases, plus reports from across the country. I kept the the-range search under eighteen just to narrow it down a bit, but once I hopped into Omega's mainframe it was pretty clear they'd done their own homework. Many files were marked 'N' and re-filed, so I assumed maybe 'N' stands for normal. The rest were marked 'P' and those were the ones I just scrolled through for you. Here I assume 'P' means paranormal." Steph waggled her eyebrows. "The dudes at Omega aren't the most imaginative types, are they?"

I wanted to laugh but my mind was focused on the photographs lining the bank of screens before me. "So apart from this, what was so huge you guys thought I'd be upset?"

Steph and Drake exchanged worried looks.

"Steph?" I said, my voice carrying an edge of impatience and annoyance.

"Okay, okay." Steph waved her hands about as if to placate me in some way. Not that it worked. "Now look. I went on a hunch and scanned a few files and ended up pulling Ari's. Seems Omega had done their own investigation on her disappearance all those years ago. But her file is active at the moment. And so are all the other files marked 'P.'"

"Active?" I asked nobody. "So, Omega's been on the case all along, and they're still on the case. But why would Ari's file be open? No one's been looking for her for a very long time."

Steph exchanged another glance with Drake and said, "So one thing you will notice is that some of the files have information about a *sigil*."

That had my attention like nobody's business. "A sigil? Like the one on Samantha's windowsill?"

Steph nodded. "Like on Samantha's windowsill, and also like on the sill of your bedroom when Ari was killed."

I looked at Drake, understanding now why he'd been so uncomfortable. He'd know this would only drive me harder to find Samantha, and he knew too that it would hurt me deep down. That knowing I might be on the trail of the same demon who'd killed my sister could possibly be a problem for me. It meant I was too close to the case. But who the hell was I supposed to pass the case on to? Not like I had a protégé hidden in one of the spare bedrooms.

"I'll screenshot some of this for you. Not taking any chances with printing or saving from secure servers I'm technically not supposed to be in." When I nodded, she said, "What are you going to do next? If that demon was able to follow you, you really need to be more careful with your projecting, and even with your jumps."

I met Drake's eyes, steeling myself for the inevitable. "He wasn't a demon. And I'm going to need to see a necromancer."

"What? You are kidding me, right?" Drake glared at me, then his eyes narrowed. "What was that thing then if it wasn't a demon?"

"He was undead. I'm guessing a powerful sorcerer, strong enough to bring himself back from the dead. But he certainly didn't return to life with all his normal looks intact. He's one ugly mother, which is why he could easily be mistaken for a demon."

"And what do you need a necromancer for, pray tell?" His eyes were chips of darkness daring me to give an unsatisfactory answer. "What about Natasha? She did the wards for the house."

"Natasha is a white witch. A spiritual mage. She wouldn't touch this kind of magic even if her own life was in danger and it could save her." I shook my head. "There is only one person I can go to right now. I need a dark magician for the spell the demons cast around Samantha."

"Why do you need a dark magician for that?" asked Steph.

"Because the demons holding Samantha used a pentagram drawn in fresh blood. The sacrifices were of living things, not of nature. And by that, I mean they used bones and blood as offerings for the spell. Nothing a white witch would want to work with." Drake was still shaking his head. And I did understand his hesitancy. Necromancers were dangerous. And you just never knew what they would want as payment.

"I still don't think a necromancer is a good idea." Drake folded his arms and scowled at me, his wide stance typical of when he got all stubborn and insistent on me.

"Then where else am I supposed to go? You see any witches or alchemists around ready to help?" My questions were met with stiff silence as both Drake and Steph glared at me. "Okay, if it will make you two feel better, I'll speak to Natasha and make sure she protects me. And maybe she will have some advice on the demons' magic."

I said the words, but I didn't have my heart in it, and from the dark look in his eyes, I suspected Drake could tell. Even Steph was too quiet as she reseated herself and pulled her keyboard toward her. Despite their misgivings, they both knew what I was up against.

I had a kid in a demon plane trapped in a dark magic circle, an undead sorcerer on my trail, and a bunch of missing persons with similarities to my sister's disappearance that I could not afford to ignore. Add that to the probability of Omega investigating my cases alongside me, and I get a bunch of chips on my shoulder that would certainly help give me the balls to go visit a necromancer.

And it wasn't like I had the luxury of putting it off either.

CHAPTER 10

MEL

After a couple of hours shut-eye, a knock on the door brought me downstairs. Detective Fulbright stood there, perspiration shining on his forehead.

I gave Fulbright an annoyed glance. "Detective."

Fulbright nodded in response. "Good morning, Ms. Morgan. Could we have a moment of your time?"

My eyes narrowed as I examined Fulbright's expression. "Fine. But I'm heading out soon, so you will have to be quick."

He'd brought someone with him. I stepped aside, allowing them to enter before closing the door and leading them into a sitting room off the entrance hall, my attention solely on the detective's partner. Dark olive skin, long silky shoulder-length hair, deep dark eyes.

"So who are you supposed to be?" I asked. "You the latest sorry sucker they found to babysit this fool?" I pointed a thumb at Fulbright, who went red.

The stranger bowed his head, a little dip that revealed a hint of his eyes behind the tops of his sunglasses, along with a tantalizing few inches of skin at his neckline—skin covered in dark swirling tattoos. My stomach tightened, and I found it a bit hard to breathe. I had to force myself to concentrate when he spoke. "My name is Saleem. I'm assigned to partner Detective Fulbright for a short period of time. I'm sort of on temporary loan." His voice was smooth, liquid gold wrapping itself around me.

He extended his hand and I took it, but instead of shaking it like a normal person would, I froze. The rush of sensations that sparked through my fingers wasn't what had caught my attention, though it was strong enough to take my breath away.

Although I was primarily a tracker, I possessed additional abilities many other trackers didn't. For instance, I was able to sense the magical ward around my house and would probably know if someone tried to tamper with it. At the moment, the mere touch of my hand to Saleem's told me he was a djinn.

I must have been silent for too long. It gave Fulbright's fury a chance to simmer. "You can give Agent Saleem his hand back and answer my damned questions," he snapped. But even as he spoke, his tone distracted me. Maybe it was the way he spoke the djinn's name, and the expression on his face as he said it, like he'd just thrown up and still had the taste of vomit in his mouth. I glared at him, then glanced back at Saleem who'd been watching me with very observant eyes. He knew I'd picked up on Fulbright's tone, but his only response was a *that's life* shrug.

I, on the other hand, wasn't calm. I was furious.

Saleem seemed to read my thoughts. "It is good to meet you, Ms. Morgan." I shivered—the nice kind. Fulbright still stood there as if waiting for something. Oh, yes, those damned questions.

"Okay, Detective, what do you need."

Fulbright cleared his throat, "What do you know about a man named Samuel Fontaine?"

I stiffened and glanced at the djinn's face. His expression darkened. Seems he disliked his partner's question as well.

"He is a friend. Is there something wrong?"

Fulbright shook his head. "No. I just wanted to get your

version of what happened to Mr. Fontaine to result in his current condition."

I shrugged. "How would I know?" Inside, I tried not to panic.

"I was under the impression he'd had a stroke," he said, his lip curling into a sneer.

"Stroke, tumor. Who knows?"

"If he'd had a brain scan, we might have an idea. Any reason why his family never sought the advice of the medical sector to help him get better?"

I stared at him. "I don't know what his family did and didn't do. Samuel is my friend." I waited as the silence grew between us. "Are we done here, Detective?"

The vein at his temple throbbed as he turned on his heel and strode to the door. I glanced at the hunky djinn and he smiled. A hot and dreamy smile that threatened to melt my insides. With that, he too walked to the front door, all the while those deep dark eyes never left my face once.

CHAPTER 11

"You aren't going anywhere without me," said Drake from behind my desk as I walked into the study after seeing the cops off. My bag hung over my shoulder, all my weapons where they were supposed to be. I was ready to go see the necromancer.

I raised an eyebrow and controlled my lips as they began to lift into a grin. Drake looked really serious but I didn't want to hurt his feelings by making him think I was making fun of him. I just said, "Playing the bodyguard now, are we?"

Drake rolled his eyes, the dark gray of them glinting. His mouth didn't turn up with a hint of a smile like it usually did. He was dead serious. "I'm coming and you don't have a say."

"You do know I can just jump and leave you behind, right?" I asked, crossing my arms, remembering too late that Drake took body language very seriously and he'd assume some kind of underlying reasoning behind my physical behavior. I knew I was right when his eyes flitted toward my crossed arms and his jaw hardened. But I didn't move. Let him think whatever he wanted.

"You could." He nodded, his expression dark. "And then I will leave."

My chest tightened. I uncrossed my arms and moved forward to place them on the desk, coming face-to-face with the gargoyle. "What's that supposed to mean?" I asked, my voice harder and more serious now.

"It means I refuse to stay with you if you keep running head-long into danger without backup," he said coldly, a darker emotion edging the timbre of his voice. "Not to mention the fact that you just did six jumps in the last few hours, two of them jumping two people. Reckless, if you ask me."

I glared at him, ignoring the mention of the jumps. I knew well enough how taxing they were on my body. "Nobody is forcing you to stay." I gritted my teeth. Why was he doing this now? Why was he delaying me when I needed to get going? I glanced at the table and tamped back the sudden urge to smile again. The surface of my work desk was littered with weapons and money. Otherworldly money. All the currencies we'd collected.

Over the years, I'd been paid with paranormal currency a few times—had a hard time saying no to people desperate to find their loved ones—even when I knew it would be damned difficult to convert. I sighed. "So what's all this?" I straightened and waved my hand at the contents of the desk.

"Are you blind?" Drake asked, his voice holding an edge of ice. Wow, okay then. He was serious. I stayed silent. "I managed to find all the paranormal money we have. It may come in handy if the necromancer wants payment."

I snorted. "What makes you think he'll want something as superficial as money?"

Drake did a double-take. "What do you think he would want then? I know you can pay them with money, so what do you mean?"

"I can't be totally sure, but from the look of the pentagram holding Samantha, I'd say he'd be asking for blood, if not a life, in exchange for his help." I watched Drake's face as he paled. His skin, a dark inky blue, turned a cool gray.

He glared at me. "So you're sure he's going to ask for blood, but you're okay to go see him?" I opened my mouth to respond but he cut me off. "Blood magic is not a game you want to play." His voice echoed ominously through my office as if it had a life of its own.

"Do I look like I have a choice? Samantha Cross's life depends on me right now. Every move I make gets me closer to releasing her, and if a visit to a necromancer and a little blood magic can get me there, then so be it."

Drake stared at me, the vein in his throat pulsing. I could tell he didn't want me to go, could see him struggling with his emotions. Then I sighed. "Fine, you can come with me. But don't get in my way. And don't get heroic or I swear I will jump you back home so fast you'll take days to remember you are still attached to your body."

He nodded solemnly and began wrapping up the foreign notes. "I don't think we'll be needing those," I said. He raised his eyes, a question in his expression. I didn't answer. Just turned and said, "Bring the weapons."

Drake followed me out to the car without a word. He strode toward the trunk, his neck stiff.

Looks like I'm in for it.

Drake was coming, but he wasn't coming quietly. Or rather, he was coming *too* quietly.

As I walked toward the driver's door, he stepped past me and got inside. When he held his palm out for the key, I handed it to him without a fuss and walked around the car to get into the passenger side. Drake glared at me as I stowed my bag and buckled up. I guessed that meant it wasn't going to be a fun ride. He put the car into gear and drove off.

I glanced around, up and down the street.

I turned my attention back to Drake and studied his profile.

Drake always stayed by my side. The last nine years. That's not to say he didn't go off on his own every now and again. But he always came back. He always came back to look out for me.

I never asked him where he went or who he saw on his trips. He was always tight-lipped about his family and friends, and to this day I still did not know how he ended up under Storm's protection.

We'd gone head-to-head a few times in the past but it was not often that I saw Drake as upset as he was today. I sighed and said, "Okay, fine, we'll visit Natasha before we go to this necromancer."

"I knew you had no intention of seeing her, despite what you said to Steph and me." Drake kept his eyes on the road. "Why the sudden change of heart?"

"No matter what you think of me, I don't like you to worry. So let's go see the white witch first. Who knows, maybe I could use a little white magic to counteract the dark."

Drake snorted, but I didn't miss the small curve of his lips as he tried not to smile. He was cute when he smiled. Not my kind of cute, though. We really needed to find Drake a girlfriend. Drake's last paramour was as dark as they came. Maybe it was time to find him someone a little nicer and a lot more permanent.

The car was silent as we made our way through streets guarded by overhanging elms and oaks. A normal street in a normal suburb just like any other. Who would imagine that a gargoyle and a mage had just driven by? I didn't break the silence, just enjoyed the quiet ride.

I only paid attention once suburb became country. I enjoyed the sights of rows and rows of corn and whatever other green stuff it was the farmers planted. At last, we turned onto an unpaved road and bounced around for at least ten minutes before we arrived at an abandoned farmhouse.

Bordered on three sides by a forest of elms and oaks, the

house looked ready to fall in on itself. Cracked and boarded-up windows dotted the front of the building, while the porch stairs teetered dangerously. A stiff breeze sent an ancient rocking chair moving back and forth eerily.

The house said *stay away* and yet I didn't listen. I grabbed my bag and shut the car door. Drake did the same, following close behind me as I tried the stairs to the porch, hoping I didn't fall through. But the floorboards were firm under my feet and I smiled. Natasha was really good at her glamour magic. So good that sometimes even I couldn't see through it unless I paid really close attention.

The air beside me shifted, and even before I looked, I knew that Drake would've gone invisible. I had always found the gargoyle's power to become invisible pretty cool. I nodded, knowing he would see me. Knowing too, especially since we had come to see the white witch, it was probably better if she didn't see him.

CHAPTER 12

I knocked lightly on the door and it opened almost immediately under my touch. I was a little startled and had to remind myself I'd come to visit a witch. Naturally, there would be magic around.

Natasha smiled up at me, honey brown eyes beaming cheerfully, the morning light catching the silvery highlights in her pale hair. "Well, hello Mel. I had a feeling I'd be seeing you soon."

"Of course, you would have a feeling." I snorted as she moved aside for me.

I entered, turning back when Natasha remained at the door, her spine stiff. *Uh-oh.* She stood on the threshold, staring out at the porch, her stillness giving me a sinking feeling.

"Now where do you think you are going?" she asked the air straight ahead of her. When she got no answer, she laughed. "Don't stand there and think I can't see you."

I grinned, wondering what Drake would do now. I could just imagine how uncomfortable he was, standing there all invisible and knowing Natasha could still see him. So much for his gargoyle magic.

The air shimmered and Drake slowly became visible. He

scowled as he stared at Natasha, although his eyes held a touch of embarrassment.

"Thank you," she said. "And now you can wait on the porch while Mel and I talk." She didn't wait for an answer. Just closed the door in his face.

I chuckled. "Drake's not going to be very happy about that."

The witch was unperturbed. "Well, unless he's come here on a personal visit, he is not coming inside. I don't allow dark creatures within the walls of my home. Not without a very good reason. And accompanying a friend is not one of them."

I glanced at the closed door. "Poor guy. All he wants is to help."

"He can help by sitting quietly on the porch and not disturbing me."

I chuckled again, giving the door another fleeting look and thinking about the angry gargoyle just beyond it. "I don't think he's going anywhere anytime soon," I said.

Natasha nodded and walked further into the hallway, her hips swaying with an unconscious grace. For a witch, she was so down-to-earth it was disconcerting. How often did you meet a powerful witch who liked jeans and t-shirts and war games? She led me into a large sitting room. On my first visit here a long, long time ago, I'd been pleasantly surprised. The house was nothing like I'd imagined a witch's home to be. Whitewashed walls, beautiful landscape paintings, antique vases and urns, and dozens of handcrafted rugs filled the rooms. I sank into a couch, leaning back against half a dozen cushions. Natasha seated herself opposite me and waited, her face serene, her white-blonde hair framing her face and hanging down to her waist.

I cleared my throat, feeling a little uncomfortable. I had figured I'd come to see Natasha, but hadn't exactly decided on what I needed from her. Not a very smart move.

"So, what can I do for you?" she asked, her expression curious, yet pleasant. It was a damned good thing this white witch liked me.

"I'm not sure," I said. "This case I'm working on, part of it involves me hiring the services of a necromancer." I didn't miss the narrowing of her eyes or the tightening of her jaw. "I'm really not sure what I'm going to need when I go to him. But I do know what I'm asking him is going to cost me."

"Why do you need to go to a necromancer?" Natasha's face darkened as she spoke.

I sighed, knowing she wouldn't agree easily. "My current case is a little girl. She's been taken by demons." The thought of Samantha alone and scared in that metal room somewhere in Dastra made my heart clench. The tightness and pain were sufficient reminders of the urgency.

Natasha shook her head, her eyes almost accusing. "But you usually come to me if you need help on your cases."

"This one's different," I said, taking a deep breath. "She's being warded with blood magic."

The white witch paled, giving her hair a run for its money. "You do realize this is serious stuff, don't you?"

I nodded. Natasha was always warning me about my cases, especially when it meant I traveled to other planes, and fought demons hand-to-hand. And here, I had a problem unequivocally different and incomparably more dangerous than any I had faced before. "Yeah, I know. But I need to find a way to get past the ward or I lose the girl."

Natasha nodded, the movement slow and unconscious as she considered my words. She knew enough about me to understand how important it was to me not to lose an innocent. She schooled her features and asked, "Was there a spell?"

"A pentagram written with blood, bones and fire inside it." I shuddered thinking about those bones and when I met Natasha's eyes, I saw she knew what they may be. "And some writing I didn't understand."

"Okay, that does sound like some serious dark magic." She rose and walked around to the window. I knew how she felt. The thought of Samantha stuck in that prison for even another day made me uneasy, restless. "Unfortunately, and as much as I hate to say it, the necromancer is your best bet for a spell to break the circle. Who are you going to see?"

"Nathaniel." The name echoed around the room like a death knell.

Natasha hissed. "He's a right bastard, that one. Evil to the core. You need to be really careful when you see him." She shook her head, her eyes darkening with worry. "I really wish you had an alternative. I'd rather you stayed as far away from Nathaniel as much as possible."

"I know. Me too." I leaned my head against the back of the sofa, sinking deeper into the cushions, the weight of the witch's concern heavy on my mind. I'd known it was a bad idea to see him, but her fear made me worry more. Then I sighed. "But I don't have a choice. So how can you help me?"

She turned to look at me, an expression of determination hardening her features. "We need to keep you safe. Make sure he can't spell you in any way."

Magic was the least of my problems when it came to the necromancer. "And when he asks for payment?" I raised an eyebrow.

"What do you have to pay him with?" She asked the question merely as a formality. I could see it in her eyes.

"What will he want?"

"Blood or a life sacrifice," she said dryly. I'd known the answer. Shouldn't have bothered to ask.

"I damned well hope he just wants the blood." I got to my feet as well, the thought of meeting Nathaniel turning my stomach.

"We just have to hope." She smiled, more a grimace than anything. Nothing to smile about. "Right, I'd better get you sorted then. You'll want a protection spell for your body and mind. And I might be able to fix you something to avoid the whole bloodletting thing."

"Really?" I was very curious. I knew what I was asking for would cost me, but if I could avoid giving the sorcerer my blood, I'd be very relieved.

Natasha nodded. "Come, let's get started." She headed out of the room without looking back. I followed, my mind whirling with worry and a touch of fear. I'd never had to break a blood curse before. The witch led me into the next room, which appeared far more modern than one would expect. White wallpaper with a pale gold-leaf imprint, an oak desk fronted by a pair of white single sofas. She waved her hand at the seats and said, "Sit, I won't be long."

She left the room and I heard her in the kitchen, glasses tinkling, fridge opening and closing. Five minutes later, she breezed into the room holding a tray. Three large glasses of lemonade sat on the silver plate and I glanced up at her. She just handed me a glass and placed another on the desk. Then she left with the third.

Curious, I went to the door and watched her as she headed to the front door and out to Drake. The hum of voices filtered toward me and I returned to my seat to sip the ice-cold drink, all the while smiling to myself. Drake would be totally flummoxed. I bet he wouldn't have expected hospitality while banished to the front porch.

Then Natasha returned, dusting her hands together as if thoroughly pleased with herself. She seated herself behind her desk and sat there for a moment, framed by white-and-gold striped curtains and a large picture window at her back. She took a long swig of her drink before heading to a set of drawers against the wall.

I didn't understand too much of what she did but I watched anyway. She selected a white marble bowl and a long purple amethyst and placed them in the center of the desk. Then she fetched a large glass pitcher of water from a table by the window. This she poured into the bowl until the water reached the brim. Then she rummaged in one of the drawers and withdrew a small brown bag, which she untied, revealing soft brown sand. She set it beside the bowl and headed to the left-hand wall, which was covered in floor-to-ceiling oak shelving. She reached for a small iron brazier, merely a metal box with four iron legs. This she placed on the table, arranging each of the items in a triangle with the iron stand closest to her and the purple stone right in the middle.

I shifted, restless. I'd been to see Natasha before and knew well enough it wouldn't be a five-minute job, but I did hope she wouldn't take too long. Poor Drake was staked out on the porch.

After the lemonade, I couldn't be certain that he'd be getting angrier by the minute. I hoped he was relaxed and waiting patiently. Anyone would prefer a calm Drake to a tetchy one. The witch fiddled in her desk drawer again and retrieved a pile of twigs tied together in a small bundle, and a long thin fire-lighter.

She placed the wood in the metal brazier and said, "Right. I want you to come closer. Wash your hands in the water." I returned my glass to the desk and headed around to stand beside her. I followed her instruction obediently, then dried my hands on the soft red towel she gave me.

"Now, take the bag and put a handful of soil at the point of the triangle." She indicated one point.

I completed the task and dusted the sand off my fingers. Then she passed me the fire-lighter and I flicked the switch a few times until I got a strong flame. It took a while for the twigs to catch alight, but I eventually got a good little fire going. I stepped back and glanced at Natasha. She nodded more to herself than anything and I handed the lighter back to her, returning to my seat while Natasha hovered over the desk.

Smoke rose from the brazier and hung about like a murky cloud at the ceiling. I blinked, my eyes beginning to sting, but

Natasha made no move to open the windows. Instead, she stood before the arrangement and raised her hands first to the ceiling, then to her breast, then to the desk. She spoke softly, a chant I didn't understand. Nor did I expect to.

What I did understand was the essence of the spell. She'd taken a piece of me for each item. Earth, Air, Fire and Water. The four elements of life and of magic. Now she stood, calling the elements to her, creating the fabric of the spell from nature itself.

My nose twitched, the smoke teasing my nostrils. I held my breath and crossed my fingers, hoping I wouldn't sneeze. Tears pooled at my lids, the haze growing thicker within the room.

Natasha seemed unaffected. I blinked again and stiffened, my eyes focusing on the white witch and the air around her. How had I not seen it before? She'd drawn a circle of protection around her, similar to the one currently shielding my house—an almost invisible bubble of magic.

Power burgeoned within the bubble and I could feel the pressure of it from where I sat, pressing against me like a living thing. Just because she was a white witch didn't mean she wasn't powerful. I watched her mouth move, her words distorted as she stood, her arms raised, encased in the protection of magic. Her chants grew louder, more intense, and my body tightened in response as I watched and waited.

The pressure grew and my ears began to pop. Natasha's brow gleamed with perspiration as she concentrated. Then, just as suddenly, the pressure eased and Natasha relaxed. She picked up the stone and dipped it into the water. Then she took a pinch of the soil, drew a line down the center of the little crystal, and placed it in the fire.

The flames danced and spat and with a sudden whoosh of air, the fire went out. Natasha reached for the cloth I'd wiped my hands on, using it to grab hold of the hot stone from inside the brazier. She began to wipe it clean as she walked to the shelves, opening a small box. She removed a little metal contraption attached to a silver chain, a piece of coiled metal designed to hold the stone. She fiddled with it, slipping the stone inside. The witch came toward me and I got to my feet and waited, unmoving as she hung the chain around my neck.

"Keep it on you at all times. It will protect you against most spells."

"Most?" I frowned, not liking the sound of that.

She nodded. "There are some spells that this protection will fail against. Like anything that uses your own blood, for example." Natasha raised an eyebrow and I nodded. Then she moved back to her desk. "There is one more thing, of course. Nathaniel will ask for blood. If he asks for a life, then leave. He will call you back because blood, any human blood, is precious to him. It strengthens his magical power and his spells. And since you are a mage, he will be all the more keen for a drop of your blood."

She sat heavily onto her chair, and from the creases on her forehead and the bow of her shoulders, I knew she was worried.

"The best way to trick him is to not use magic."

I frowned. That was new. "No magic?"

"Yes." She opened the drawer in front of her and withdrew a long object wrapped in leather and twisted it to reveal the hollow handle. "This is a trick knife. The kind used by fake magicians. See how the inside of it is hollow? With a little pressure, the point of the knife opens to allow the blood to leak out. It will look like you are cutting yourself."

Natasha handed the knife over to me. After a quick inspection, I gave it back. "So. Whose blood are we using?"

Natasha laughed, the tension in her face easing a little. "Don't worry. I am not donating. We will use blood from my milking cow."

I raised my eyebrows but didn't question her. She knew what she was doing. I hoped.

CHAPTER 13

Saleem's mind was on the too-sexy-for-her-own-good SoulTracker. He'd heard she was feisty and strong, but nobody had mentioned she was hot. The precinct hummed with low voices and the tapping of keyboards as Saleem watched Fulbright make his way to his desk, coffee cup in one hand and a file in the other. Chances were, that file was another abduction case.

Fulbright's face was pinched and red, skin sagging and dark under his eyes. He reached his desk opposite Saleem's, tugged the gaudy orange tie from his neck and unbuttoned his collar. It did nothing to improve the thick lines of his neck. The detective grunted, then took a swig from his cup.

He drew the back of his hand across his mouth, slapped the file on the desk and proceeded to rifle through his In-tray with his unoccupied hand. Most of the papers were tossed aside. Then he returned his attention to the file. In all that time, he hadn't looked at Saleem once.

"Rough night?" Saleem asked, trying to keep the scorn out of his voice. He disliked the detective but Saleem wouldn't let odious man know it.

"Yeah." Fulbright's gaze remained on his file.

Sure, his rough night was all in his head. Fulbright kept too many things too close to his chest. Saleem decided to encourage a better answer. He leaned forward and asked, "Anything happen?"

Fulbright looked up and studied him for a moment, his expression cold and impersonal. Then he replied. "Yeah, I've got a few things to investigate before I'm sure. I'll let you know." He returned his gaze to the file.

Bastard.

Saleem ground his jaw as he stared at the top of Fulbright's head. The man rubbed him the wrong way, and that was dangerous. Magic pulsed through Saleem's veins but he tamped it down. He was here to watch the man, not incinerate his ass.

The phone rang, pulling Saleem safely back to reality. Fulbright glanced up at him, giving the phone a pointed look. Saleem gritted his teeth and picked up the receiver.

It turned out to be a call from missing persons. A teenage boy was missing. At last, a chance to watch Fulbright in action. He took a few notes and when he put the phone down, the older man looked at him, his gaze hard and expectant. "It's a new missing persons' report."

"Where?" Fulbright sat up straight, raising his eyebrows at Saleem, urging him to answer quickly.

"Manchester Heights. Seventeen-year-old male. Name's Ethan Reed."

"How long?"

"Since this morning. Could be last night. Parents haven't seen him since he went to bed last night."

Fulbright was already rising, chugging down the last of his now-cold coffee. He flung the cup at the wastepaper basket, not caring that it fell short and rolled into the aisle. He grabbed his file and headed out of the office, swiftly avoiding the still-rolling cup.

Saleem remained close on his heels. When he jumped into the

car beside Fulbright, the detective gave him a sour glare. But he said nothing, clearly resigned to his new partner. He shifted into gear and sped off down the street. Saleem was silent as they wove through the city, soon passing through residential areas that got poorer the further they went. He wasn't in the mood to talk to Fulbright. What he really wanted to do was punch the man in the face.

They arrived at the house—an old weatherboard building with peeling paint and an unkempt front yard. A police cruiser sat outside, lights flashing, while an officer spoke to a man at the front door. The cop glanced over his shoulder as they approached, and Saleem hid a smile at the pained expression on his face the moment his gaze fell on Fulbright.

The detective seemed oblivious as he marched up the cracked sidewalk and headed for the door. Saleem winced, hoping Fulbright wouldn't come on too strong. The man at the door—most likely the father—looked upset enough.

Saleem hurried after Fulbright, greeting the other police officer with a nod as he passed him on his way to his vehicle. Saleem approached the entrance to the house and introduced himself just as the detective stopped speaking. Fulbright gave him a narrow stare, as if he'd hoped Saleem had conveniently disappeared.

If only he knew.

"Come in, detectives." Reed waved them inside and Saleem watched Fulbright's spine stiffen at the assumption that Saleem was also a detective. But he didn't bother to correct the man.

A woman entered the lounge, curly red hair mussed, eyes red. Lines tracked her wan face deeply and her gray complexion spoke of hours of worry and inconsolable tears. She stared at them, her expression almost indifferent. As if some part of her had already given up.

On a hunch, Saleem studied the house for magic or charms but came up empty. He wanted to ask to see the boy's room but hesitated, preferring not to piss Fulbright off any more than necessary.

"Please sit," the father said. When Fulbright sat, the man held his hand out. "I'm Robert Reed, this is my wife Betty." The detective flushed as he rose to take the man's hand, giving it a perfunctory shake. He nodded at the wife and resumed his seat, fishing his notebook from his inside jacket pocket. Saleem shook hands with both parents and remained standing.

Fulbright went over the time they last saw their son, what his mood was, if he had any problems at school—all the usual questions. Listening with half an ear, Saleem drifted toward the inner hallway which he assumed led to the boy's room. Three doors led off the passage and all were open, allowing weak light to shine on the worn and threadbare carpeting.

Once he got the lay of the place, Saleem went to the front door, glancing back at Fulbright, who looked up at him, dislike clear on his face. Saleem headed for the car and got in, shutting the door hard enough for the detective to hear the sound from inside.

Then, with a glance up at the house to make sure nobody was watching, Saleem simply disappeared in a flash of amber embers. And appeared again at the furthest end of the passage within the Reed home.

Fortunately, the boy's room was immediately to his left and he stepped inside, moving with extra care, afraid of making any loose floorboards creak. Inside the room, he kept one ear out on the drone of Fulbright's voice and the short, sharp answers of the Reeds. They'd taken an instant dislike to the detective. Must have been his interrogatory demeanor.

The kid's room screamed *boy*. Dark blue curtains, a rickety bookshelf stacked with comics. A football lay in a corner, an old computer sat at the desk beside the window. The bed was unmade, the sheets thrown off as if he'd risen in a hurry. The window sash was raised, the curtain shifting in the breeze.

Saleem wanted to rule out anything paranormal from this possible abduction. He couldn't sense any spells here. And if there had been a paranormal presence like demons or wraiths, their scents would certainly have faded over the last few hours. They really should have been on the scene this morning.

There was nothing in the room. Nothing to indicate anything unusual or abnormal had happened. Nothing to indicate anything paranormal, either. Saleem was disappointed to leave without any clues, but from the rising voices in the sitting room, it seemed Fulbright was ending his interview. And any detective worth his salt would head down for a thorough inspection of the boy's room, so Saleem needed to get the hell out of there.

Just as he was about to transport himself back to the car, his eye caught something strange on the windowsill. He grabbed his phone and stepped closer, then snapped a couple of pictures and disappeared in a flash of orange sparks just as the parents entered the room with Fulbright close on their heels.

Saleem reappeared in the interior of the car, his phone in hand. He stared immediately at the screen. The image chilled his blood. Although the windowsill had appeared clean, Saleem was blessed with a secondary sight, courtesy of his demon blood. And dark sight allowed him to see the demonic sigil drawn on the sill.

Saleem's gut clenched. There was more to these kidnappings than met the eye. He held in his hand proof demons were involved in this particular boy's abduction, but what about all the other missing persons Fulbright was investigating? How many of them were demonic as well? And what, if anything, did Mel Morgan know about it?

He glanced over at the house, wondering for the first time if Fulbright had really been onto something. Maybe he had known there was more to these disappearances. Saleem shook his head, trying to absorb the turn this case had taken. This information would be valuable to Omega, but for once he hesitated to pass it on. He had his own problems, and to solve them, he planned on looking to the sexy Ms. Morgan. If anyone could help him, she could.

Fulbright left the Reeds' house and hurried down the path to the car, almost tripping over the uneven concrete. He threw himself into the car, waves of negative energy rolling off him as he gunned the engine.

"What's wrong? Find anything?" Saleem knew he was expected to ask something. He was slowly learning more about the way the man worked. He liked to trail information like little crumbs.

"Nothing." Fulbright grunted. "I searched the room and came up with nothing. How is that possible?" His eyes glittered with fury and his fingers tightened dangerously on the steering wheel.

"So you think he's a runaway?" Saleem offered the option.

The detective glanced at Saleem, irritated. "He didn't take anything with him. Not even his wallet or his money. What kid runs away without at least taking something with him?"

Good question. Fulbright wasn't stupid. So he knew it was most likely an abduction.

"We need to keep this under wraps. I don't want that Morgan woman finding out about it."

"How would she find out?" Saleem asked, curious as to how the man came to his conclusions. Why would he immediately focus on Morgan?

"Who the fuck knows. Every case involving abduction, she's there afterward when we close it, unsolved. I think someone is feeding her information." Bitterness simmered in his tone.

"But that's after the case has been declared unsolved, right?" Saleem pointed out. Fulbright seemed so eager to point a finger at Morgan. What he didn't know was that it was his own Chief who willingly worked with paranormal intelligence, who regularly fed Mel Morgan unsolved cases.

"Yeah, whatever. It's like she's psychic. How the hell does she do it?"

"So, she's like a psychic private detective or something." Saleem met the detective's eyes.

Fulbright snorted, although he flushed. "Some private detective." Then, Fulbright drove off, eyes on the road, refusing to discuss anything further.

Saleem could understand Fulbright's frustrations where Morgan was involved. But it solidified his decision even more.

If anyone could help him find his own missing person, it would be Mel Morgan. Now, all he had to do was to get her to agree to do it.

CHAPTER 14

On the ride to see Nathaniel, Drake was a little too quiet.

I glanced at him but he kept his eyes on the road as he drove. "Hey, sorry about Natasha. I didn't expect her to banish you to the porch."

"I was fine." He bit the words out. Good sign. If he wasn't, his entire body would have said so.

"The lemonade was nice of her." I waited for a reaction.

"Yeah."

I frowned. "What's wrong?" My tone was hard and impatient. He'd already had one tantrum and I'd given in to him. Now, I was getting annoyed with his reticence.

"What's wrong? This whole thing is wrong. Nathaniel is too powerful." His fingers tightened on the steering wheel. "I just have a bad feeling about this."

I shook my head. "Bad feeling or not, I still have to go. Samantha Cross is waiting, and I don't think we can afford for her to be left much longer. Who knows what they will do to her . . . we have to rescue her."

Drake nodded and sighed. "I understand that. I do. It's just that my gut thinks this is a bad idea."

I sighed. "I know. My gut agrees. Making deals with death sorcerers is not exactly my cup of tea. But he's the only one I know of who can help me with a spell against the blood magic ward." I sighed again. "He's my only option right now."

"Okay then, let's do this. You ready?" He glanced at me, a worrying question in his eyes.

I snorted. "As ready as I will ever be."

~

THE REST of the drive was silent as Drake drove through the streets, passing blue-collar and white-collar residential areas until we reached what qualified as gold-collar, as far as I was concerned. We slid quietly through the streets, hemmed in by palatial mansions that loomed over high walls and dense tree-filled fences. When Drake drew up in front of a set of towering wrought-iron gates, I was sure he'd gotten the wrong address.

"Is this the right place?" I laughed, looking at Drake as if he was kidding.

"Yup, this is the address." Then he glanced at me, a dark look in his eyes. "At least I know you've never been to see Nathaniel before."

I glared at him but turned my attention back to the gates. Not the best time for a spat. A speakerphone sat on a metal pole to the left of the drive. Drake got out of the car and went to it, speaking into the box. I watched the gargoyle, wondering why he was so accommodating all of a sudden. Not too long ago he'd been trying to talk me out of coming, and now he was getting me access to the sorcerer.

As Drake returned to the car, the gates began to swing open. My stomach clenched as we moved forward, closer to Nathaniel. Just because I was determined to see the man didn't mean I thought it was a fabulous idea. I bit my lip as Drake maneuvered the car along the winding drive. He stopped on the gravel beside the stairs leading to a wide porch. A pair of white Grecian columns flanked the entrance, rising all the way to the roof.

Impressive.

As we left the car, I scanned the grounds; landscaped and manicured gardens seemed to stretch endlessly all around the house. We hurried up the steps and I pressed the buzzer while Drake fidgeted beside me.

"What did you tell them?"

"Just that you needed to see Nathaniel and does he have some time available."

I raised an eyebrow. "Very polite."

"I'm trying to play a part here, okay?"

"And what part is that?"

"Resigned sidekick?" His voice held an edge of ice so I backed off. More important things to think about. But as soon as we got home, I would have to sit Drake down for a nice long talk.

The door opened, putting an end to our silent standoff. The thin, tall man staring at us wore a black suit, including a small black bow tie, his skin pasty as if he had forgotten what the sun was. "I believe you wish to see Master Nathaniel?"

I blinked at his accent, so English and so posh. Everything about this address seemed so wrong. I'd come here to meet a necromancer. Where was the shadiness, the house with an air of gloom? I was disappointed that not a single dark and angry cloud wafted over the property.

"Yes, I do." I nodded, feeling awkward. What else was I supposed to say?

"Follow me, please." The butler led us into a large and airy lounge and gave a small bow. "The Master will be with you short-ly." Then he left, giving us a final glance that made me certain he didn't like our presence too much. His cold eyes slithered over me before he turned and stalked out of the room.

"Nice guy, huh?" I asked Drake, more to break the weird

silence than a desire for conversation. My stomach writhed, as my nerves couldn't decide what to do with themselves.

Drake grunted. "Be careful what you say and how you say it."

I raised my eyebrows again. No nonsense, just a warning? Drake must be worried.

Footsteps sounded in the hall and a man entered the room. He was resplendent in a black morning suit, his dove-gray lapels perfectly complementing his salt-and-pepper hair. I don't know how I'd pictured Nathaniel, but it certainly wasn't this elegant, aging gentleman.

His fingers gleamed with silver and gold rings, and his ears were studded with stones. I swallowed as he strode closer, a hard glint in his bright green eyes. He had an odd look on his face, as if he wanted to say something then stopped himself. Then it was gone and I chalked it up to my jitters.

He halted before me and held out his hand. "Nathaniel Hawker. How can I help you?"

Okay, so this *was* the necromancer I was here to meet. Nothing here was what I expected. I took his hand. I didn't want to, but I didn't have much of a choice either. "Mel Morgan. And this is Drake Darvon."

He gave my hand a swift, firm shake and then moved on to Drake. I'd heard it said you can tell a man by his handshake but right here, right now, I knew you couldn't tell a thing about Nathaniel from his grip. You'd be forgiven to think he was just a wealthy, eccentric old man. But he wasn't. Energy rolled off him in waves.

Magical and dark.

An ominous silence hung over the room and I turned to Drake and the necromancer beside me. Nathaniel still held his hand, staring at Drake, his green eyes sharp and cold. He took a breath, then let go of Drake's hand, seemingly changing his mind about saying anything to the gargoyle.

What was it with Drake today? First Natasha and now the sorcerer?

Nathaniel turned away from Drake, piercing me with his cold eyes. "Please sit," he said, waving us at the long black leather couch behind us. He sat opposite us on the matching sofa. He leaned forward with his elbows on his knees and stared intently at me. "So, tell me why you have come." His words were short and precise, as if he wanted to waste not a single minute with us.

At first, I hesitated, unsure of how to put my request into words. Then I decided I might as well be clear and upfront about it, no beating around the bush. "I need a counter-spell. It's for a demon circle created with blood. My understanding is a circle like that can only be created with dark magic."

"That is correct." Nathaniel nodded, his eyes never leaving my face. "Can you describe the circle to me in as much detail as possible?"

I glanced at Drake, his eyes revealing a warning, but I returned my gaze to the sorcerer. I described the blood circle and watched as the necromancer's face grew darker, the skin at his eyes tightening. I tamped down the urge to frown as I took in his reaction. He seemed much too upset. Too affected by my description.

"Have I said something wrong?" I asked, not taking my eyes off his face.

He blinked as if seeing me for the first time. "No, no. There is nothing wrong." And then he fell silent.

I pressed further. "You seem upset about something."

He shook his head, but his eyes darkened, and I could almost feel his anger. "No, not upset," he said. "It's just that what you have described to me is really dark magic, and I'm wondering where you would have come across something like this."

I narrowed my eyes as I looked at him. "Does it really matter?" I asked.

Nathaniel's gaze went from me, and then to Drake. He got to

his feet and said, "I guess it doesn't really matter. After all, what matters right now is you came to me because you need something, so let me see what I can do about it."

He spoke so formally that for a minute, I was concerned.

Then Nathaniel moved toward the door and said, "Would you like to follow me? It's best we do this in private."

I nodded, and he spun on his heel and walked straight out of the door. Drake and I followed him, keeping close as he led us further into the house. Dark wood paneling covered the walls halfway up. He came to a set of stairs that led to a lower floor, probably the basement. I hesitated for a split second before following him.

Of course, the necromancer would have an underground lair. What else should I have expected?

He descended the stairs slowly and at the bottom came to a stop in front of a pair of wooden doors set into a carved archway. As I neared it, I felt a wave of dark energy batter my body. His lair was protected by a dark magic spell, so strong I could taste blood. I needn't have been concerned though, as Nathaniel would allow us to enter, thus ensuring the spell didn't shatter us to pieces.

He touched the door and it swung open silently. The scent of sulfur mixed strangely with incense, tickling my nose as we followed the necromancer inside.

Now this was more like it.

Whether the mansion above was built on a warren of subterranean tunnels, I did not know. All I knew was I was now in a cave, the walls of which glistened with a strange shimmering liquid.

Nathaniel waved us inside, heading toward a gigantic wooden desk piled with bottles and bowls filled with an array of strange liquids. A timely reminder that we were essentially dealing with an alchemist gone bad.

Nathaniel Hawker had originally begun his magical career as

an alchemist, developing his talents in sorcery through the years. He'd had an illustrious career, been a powerful mage admired and respected by those who knew what he was capable of.

Unfortunately, he seemed to have lost the plot along the way, delving into the darkest of magics, bringing the dead back to life. Nobody doubted he was good at what he did. I didn't doubt it either. I just preferred not to meet any of his zombie monsters.

Ever.

The room pulsed with energy, a magical power that had a sense of darkness to it that even *I* could feel. A glance over at Drake, and it was clear he sensed it too. But we'd come this far. And from the looks of it, we weren't going anywhere until this transaction was completed.

"Can you come forward, Ms. Morgan?" Nathaniel's voice boomed across the room, the sound echoing against the stone walls.

I blinked, startled at the power behind his voice. Looking over at him, I saw he'd donned a black robe that shrouded his face. All I could see were the shadowy angles of his jaw and the dark hollows of his eye sockets. I tamped down the urge to shudder and walked over to him.

No use chickening out now.

CHAPTER 15

MEL

As soon as I stood before him, he hissed, raising his hands as if to protect himself from me.

Then he laughed, the sound harsh against my ears. "I see you have secured magical protection." He laughed again and the hairs on the back of my neck rose. "If we are to continue, I will request you remove the talisman and leave it outside this room."

I frowned and glanced over at Drake, whose face had darkened with concern. This was unexpected, but it was understandable he would not welcome other magic into his private lair. I hesitated, then dragged the leather band over my neck, handing it to Drake, who took it outside for me. I wasn't too worried, as the magic would last for a few hours even if I removed the charm.

And Nathaniel realized it as soon as I turned back to him. His face twisted with anger, but he seemed to come to some internal decision. He took a deep breath and said nothing. Just beckoned me to move closer.

When I got to the table's edge, he held out a black stone bowl that resembled a mortar. He met my gaze, his green eyes blazing. "I need your blood."

I glanced from the bowl, to his face, and back again. Then I reached for the knife at my side.

Nathaniel looked at the knife, then at me. I looked at him waiting for an okay. Let him think he had the upper hand by giving me permission. As soon as he nodded, I unsheathed the knife and placed the tip on the vein at my wrist. I pressed, hoping the blade wouldn't fail and end up slicing into me.

But I need not have worried. As I placed pressure on the blade, a thin line of red appeared on my skin. I glanced up at the necromancer. He watched me closely, his hands touching the table's edge as if it was all that stopped him from lunging at the bowl to get his hands on the blood. He met my eyes and raised his chin, giving me another nod. I wasn't sure what that meant. Was he happy with the blood? Was he giving me permission to continue?

I turned my attention back to my wrist and continued the even pressure on my skin. The blood leaked, bright red and fresh, dripping into the bowl far too slowly for my liking. I wanted it all over and done with, but of course I had no choice but to wait until the show was over. Someone came to stand beside me and I glanced over, expecting to see Drake.

My heart thudded as I looked up into a pair of icy green eyes. Nathaniel. He'd moved so quietly I hadn't realized until he was already there. I really should have been more aware of my surroundings.

Now, fear began to bubble within my veins as he remained there, silent as the dead he reanimated. The scent of his perfume tickled my nostrils. Something musky and sexy sweet and totally not suited to his dark arts.

He leaned over me, staring intently into the bowl, watching the rich red blood pooling in the base of the mortar. Then he sniffed at the bowl and a rush of terror spiked through me. He was smelling the blood.

That was not supposed to happen.

My heart thudded against my ribcage so hard I was certain he'd hear it. Could he smell the difference between human and bovine blood? He bent closer, his nose hovering above the bowl, and breathed in the scent of the blood—and I knew I was in deep shit.

He growled as he straightened and turned slowly to face me. A vein pulsed in his neck and his face hardened. "You would dare to cheat me?" His voice was low and dangerous and sent chills up and down my spine.

He reached for me, his fingers gnarled and twisted, wrapping his hands around my neck. And then he squeezed. His eyes bulged, and I could see the white of his sclerae gleaming. He lifted me off the ground, the weight putting more pressure on his grip.

I struggled for air but couldn't take a breath. His fingers pressed deep into my throat and I blinked in terror. Stupid. At the time, using the fake knife had seemed like a good idea. Now, not so much.

An angry roar emanated from behind me and Drake slammed into Nathaniel, sending him crashing into the table. Dozens of bottles and books slid across the desk. Nathaniel flailed, his hands reaching out to grip the edge of the desk and avoid sliding across the surface.

As he moved, his fingers hit the bowl containing the blood, sending it flying off the table. It landed on the ground with a harsh crack and split in half, spilling cow's blood all over the stone floor.

I coughed, bending over and clutching my throat. I struggled to take a breath.

"Mel!" Drake yelled. "Run."

I stared at him. How could I leave without the spell? I had no other way of saving Samantha. That moment of hesitation was all

Nathaniel needed. A dark blast of power flew at Drake, thick and solid, an opaque shadow that hit him square in the chest, lifting him off the ground.

He flew backward at least five feet before hitting the stone wall so hard I was sure I heard an ominous crack. He slid to the floor and groaned, then pushed himself back up.

He rubbed his head and held his hand up, then frowned at the streaks of blood marking his palm. His face darkened and he stood up, holding onto the wall.

I wanted to help him but with Nathaniel facing me, one hand outstretched in my direction, I knew he wouldn't hesitate to deliver the same treatment to me if I moved. Not that I was afraid of him. But I needed to be awake and aware, not knocked off my feet and unconscious.

Nathaniel laughed, the sound echoing harshly around the room. Drake glowered but the sorcerer paid him little attention. "So, Ms. Morgan, I do believe it's time you made a decision."

I frowned. "What decision is that?" He had my curiosity piqued.

"You need to make a decision right now. No waiting, no time to consider." He fell silent abruptly.

"What's the decision?" I asked sharply, irritated he was dragging this out.

Nathaniel smiled, then glanced over at Drake. The necromancer flicked his hand in my friend's direction and I gasped as Drake rose so suddenly up into the air that if I blinked I would have missed it. He now lay horizontal and floated in the air, five feet off the ground. I glared at Nathaniel. "What the hell are you doing to him?"

"What anyone would do if they were duped by the likes of you. I am using my advantages." He smiled smugly.

"What do you want?" I shouted at him, uncaring if I angered him or hurt his feelings. They were the least of my concerns right now.

"Your blood," he said, his voice soft and cold as it slithered down my spine. He was going to force me to give my blood. I should have known.

I stared at him. He stared back.

"Don't even try to think of a way out. It will cost you your friend's life."

I hesitated and he saw me, sensed it. Somehow, he knew. "Very well, perhaps you need a little more incentive." Nathaniel waved his hand, and I expected Drake to go flying across the room again, but he didn't move.

Then he grunted, as if in deep pain. He called my name and my stomach twisted as I saw what Nathaniel had done to him. Drake's skin began to darken in color, changing from his normal dark gray skin tone to a lifeless shade of gray.

The color of stone.

Drake tried to speak but he couldn't move his lips. He just watched me, eyes wide. I knew what he was saying. *Don't give him your blood.* I glanced at the necromancer, who turned to smile at me, his teeth gleaming white and making him look like a grinning puppet.

"Still have doubts, Ms. Morgan?" He knew he had me right where he wanted.

I stared at Drake, who was now solid stone. What had I allowed to happen? But Drake had insisted on coming, he'd been certain he would help protect me. And look what it had gotten him. Fury rose within me and my fingers curled into tight fists at my side.

"Come now. The blood, if you please." Nathaniel's voice penetrated my thoughts.

I didn't want to. My chest tightened with fear. Natasha's and Drake's dire warnings rang in my ears. The sorcerer clicked his tongue and Drake began to drop straight to the stone floor. Terror flooded my veins.

"Stop!" I screamed, my hand reaching out as if I could halt

Drake's fall. If he hit the ground, he would shatter into too many pieces. He'd be dead for sure.

I glared at Nathaniel, my eyes filled with tears as frustration, anger, and fear entwined into an almost tangible fury.

Nathaniel smiled. "I am tired of these games, Ms. Morgan." He glanced over at Drake. "So, my dear, do you want me to convince you more?" Nathaniel raked me with his cold eyes.

"Fine," I said, my voice shaking. "Fine. I'll do what you want. Just don't harm him."

Nathaniel nodded, his expression pleasant and friendly. "Very good. I hate playing these games." Then he smiled, his teeth gleaming in the dull light of the room. "You know, this was not necessary at all."

I said nothing. Just stared at him coldly, wondering again why I had ever thought this was a good idea. Drake had warned me. And now his life was in danger.

Anger rippled through me, spurring me to move toward the table. I just wanted to get it over and done with and get Drake home. I prayed whatever Nathaniel had done to him was reversible.

The necromancer moved toward the table as I bent over and released the knife strapped to my ankle. I hesitated, looking around for a clean receptacle. He placed a clear glass bowl on the table in front of me. He was also eager to get this over and done with.

Nathaniel placed a hand on my arm as I moved to press the knife onto my wrist. He grabbed my hand, picking the knife out of my palm and bringing it close to his eyes, turning it over and inspecting it. Then, without a word, he returned it to me and took one step back.

I glanced at him, sure he could see the hatred in my eyes. But it didn't seem to have any effect on him. Considering his occupation, he probably had a large contingent of haters.

Moving my attention back to the bowl, I placed the knife on

my wrist, bracing for the pain. I pressed the blade and watched as the tip sliced into my skin, as red blood welled from the incision.

I held my hand over the bowl, allowing the blood to drip slowly into it. The bowl filled far too slowly for my liking, but I had no choice. I was not about to cut myself deeper—or anywhere else—just to satisfy Nathaniel. Slow would have to do.

At last, when it seemed there was enough blood in the bowl for the necromancer, I turned my hand over and placed a finger on the cut to stall the bleeding. I glanced up at Nathaniel and he nodded.

And I was glad that about half a cup of my blood was enough for him. I had no idea what I would've done had he wanted more.

"Now can you release Drake?" I asked, my tone cold and hard. I wasn't in the mood for niceties.

Nathaniel laughed, the sound high pitched and irritating to my inner ear. "Of course, I can't, my dear."

"What the hell do you mean?" I asked, my voice vibrating with anger. "You said if I gave you my blood, you would release him."

"I never promised any such thing," said the sorcerer, eyes gleaming, a smile curling his lip. "The blood is, of course, the payment for the spell. Nothing more."

Fear rippled up and down my spine as I stared at the sorcerer. "What do you want?"

"Ah, that is such a loaded question, my dear. What is it that I want? I want so many things. But far too many of those things I will never get."

I didn't have time to listen to his crap. I was furious. "So you just take what you want?"

"But of course, my dear; how else would you suppose I get it?" Nathaniel's face was serious as he looked at me. I blinked. I didn't particularly care about what the necromancer wanted that he never got. I wasn't in the mood to get to know him any better. Never would be in the mood.

"Quit the games, Nathaniel," I said coldly. "Tell me what you want in exchange for Drake's life." I glanced over at Drake, who still hung in the air. He'd been totally transformed into stone, his eyes no longer urging me to go.

"I want you to steal a portal key." His eyes challenged me.

CHAPTER 16

"You what?"

"Come now, Ms. Morgan. Don't pretend with me. I know quite a bit about you." Nathaniel leaned forward and picked up the glass bowl. As he walked around the table, the blood sloshed back and forward.

I swallowed, suddenly afraid of what he was about to ask me, just as afraid as I was about what he was going to do with my blood. When he reached the opposite side of the table, he set the bowl down and met my eyes again. "You don't have to pretend here. I know you can teleport."

I raised my eyebrows, shock filtering through me. How the hell did he know that? "What?" The smartest thing I could do right now was to feign ignorance.

Nathaniel laughed. "Oh, my dear. You may not exactly be famous, but in certain circles your name is very well-known. Which is probably one of the reasons why I'm not going to kill you for trying to cheat me."

He paused and leaned to the side, opening one of his desk drawers. He took something out and held it toward me. I silenced a gasp as he opened his palm and revealed a portal key.

"I'm sure you've seen one of these before. Although perhaps you wouldn't really need it, considering. This particular one doesn't work for me, of course. And a certain High Priestess has refused to fashion one for me. So now, I have to resort to you."

"Now where the hell am I supposed to find something like that?" I asked, although I knew very well where I could get one. "Why would you need one? Aren't all your magic and spells enough to part the Veil whenever you want?"

"You are right, my dear. My magic and spells are strong enough for me to part the Veil wherever and whenever I want. But you see, it takes a lot of energy out of me and I am not getting any younger. A few keys will make my life much easier."

I squeezed my fist, anger filtering through me. I winced as the cut burned at my wrist. Blood welled to the surface and I placed a thumb on the incision, pressing firmly.

"So where is it you want me to get the key from?" I asked, determined not to make things too easy for him. My back was turned to him, but I'd bet Drake still hovered in the air behind me. I also knew I wouldn't let Nathaniel get away with what he had done to Drake.

"Don't play games with me. You know exactly where to get the keys from. Get them for me. Bring them back to me and your friend will be returned to you alive."

Nathaniel raised an eyebrow at me. He knew I really didn't have a choice, and he seemed to enjoy the fact. But I really couldn't blame him. I'd tried to cheat him. He saw an opportunity. Now he had me by the cojones. And I couldn't do anything about it. Drake's life hung in the balance. And I really couldn't trust Nathaniel.

I glanced back over my shoulder and stared at Drake. So many things to do, so little time. Samantha waited for me. Who knew how long she had? Or what the demons had in store for her. Could I afford to wait any longer to retrieve her? At that moment, I made a decision that I prayed Drake would forgive me for. I turned back to Nathaniel.

"Is he still alive?" My eyes narrowed at Nathaniel. "Is he okay? Will he be okay once he is normal again?"

Nathaniel nodded. "Your friend is perfectly fine. He is alive. Stone is part of his nature, so believe me, he has no problem being in this form. The only problem he has is, unlike his normal transformations, he is unable to turn back to human form unless I allow it."

"Can he hear me?"

"Yes. He is fully aware of what is going on around him."

I turned again to face Drake, heart thudding against my ribs. I hoped he would understand my choice. "I will fetch the portal keys for you." Behind me, Nathaniel laughed gleefully. "But I will only do it once I'm finished with my mission. And that spell of yours had better work."

"What did you say?" His voice was harsh, the sound clattering against the walls.

"I will get you your keys, but you will have to wait. There is someone whose life is in danger. And I need to save her now."

Nathaniel chuckled. "What kind of friend are you? What do you think Drake would say about this?"

"I know exactly what Drake would have to say about this. He would want me to go and save the girl." I crossed my fingers and hoped that was true. My stomach clenched. What would I do if that wasn't what Drake really wanted? I put the thought out of my head. I had to believe that Drake would agree with me. He knew how important Samantha's life was.

"Very well." Nathaniel's eyes gleamed. "I will wait. But don't make me wait too long. Or your friend here will meet with a convenient accident and when you return, you will need a broom to sweep up his remains."

Fear pooled in my gut, solid and painful. But I refused to let him see it. "Don't you worry about it. I will be back soon. And if you so much as damage a hair on Drake's head, I promise you that I will make you pay."

Nathaniel laughed. "I'm not afraid of you, little girl." Then he glanced back behind me. "Do what you have to do and get back here fast. Don't play any games with me. You will not like the price for failure."

I didn't answer. Just looked down at the bowl of blood and prayed it would not come back to bite me. I glanced up; Nathaniel looked pretty proud of himself. "Let's get on with it. How about you hold up your end of the bargain. I've given you my blood. Now can I please have the spell?"

Nathaniel's smile faltered. He gritted his teeth and raised an eyebrow at me. "Very well." He headed to a set of shelves against the far wall and rummaged amongst the bottles and books. At last, he returned with a brass dish. He placed it on the table and poured a third of the blood I had donated into it. I raised an eyebrow in challenge, but he wasn't looking. I was surprised he was going to actually use my blood for the spell.

He took the brass dish and walked around the desk to an open space beside it. A large pentagram was carved into the stone floor. Again, I was surprised to find that he used normal magic. But it shouldn't have surprised me. All magic was magic to begin with. It was the user's decision to go dark or light.

Nathaniel placed the brass bowl at the center of the pentagram and stood back.

He raised his hands and began to chant, the sound echoing ominously around the room, making the hairs on the back of my neck rise.

Bright blue flames began to flicker along the outer circle of the pentagram. Nathaniel chanted louder and the flames grew stronger and higher. Perspiration dotted his forehead. It seemed the magic was taking its toll on his body.

At last, his voice dropped to a low murmur. He hung his head back as if staring at the ceiling, but his eyes saw nothing. They were blank. They rolled back into his eye sockets, the whites of his eyes gleaming.

He remained that way, so still I began to get scared. How dangerous was this spell of his anyway? Suddenly his head snapped forward and a bright blue flame streamed out from the ball of blood. I flinched, but managed to stay in place, staring at my blood, now burning with blue fire.

The flame rose higher, almost as tall as Nathaniel. He still remained in his trance. I couldn't take my eyes off the strange fire. It was a good thing I didn't, as I would've missed the shadows.

They roiled from each corner of the pentagram, whirling in the air. The dark streaks coiled around and around, as if reaching for each other. Nathaniel's chanting grew louder. And I shivered.

The shadows met in the center of the pentagram, directly above my burning blood. They coiled into each other, forming a solid column of blackness that flew toward the bowl of blood on the ground.

I tensed, expecting an explosion, but nothing happened. The pillar of shadow just streamed into the center of the fire in the bowl, straight into the blood. The deep red liquid began to swirl into a whirlpool, spiraling until the middle of the liquid fell, sinking deeper into the bowl.

The shadow sped toward the depression and disappeared into the blood. As I watched, darkness seeped into the red, spinning and eddying. Streaks of black and red mingled ominously with each other, mixing and blending until red faded to utter darkness and all I saw was a bowl of churning black goop.

I shuddered. That's what happens when SoulTracker blood mixes with necromancer magic.

Nathaniel fell silent and as his voice faded, so did the flames. They danced, rising and falling until they grew smaller and smaller. I breathed in, tensed for what would happen next.

Nathaniel took a step forward and the column of shadows fell straight into the bowl, snuffing out the blue flames, which disappeared in a puff of white smoke, leaving behind the burning bowl.

He picked up the bowl, headed straight for his desk and set it on the table, then rummaged around amongst the shattered and broken remains of tubes, decanters, and metal stands. He finally emerged with three small tubes, each with a screw-top lid topped with a metal loop.

He glanced up at me as if to make sure I was still there. But I had no intention of leaving without my spell.

I waited as he used a small ladle to dispense some of the spelled blood into the three vials. He screwed the lids back on firmly, then held the tubes in his hand, staring at them intently.

What was he doing? More dead mojo, or was he having second thoughts?

My fingers itched to grab my knife but I waited. Nathaniel already had the upper hand. I doubted he would be so stupid, especially since he wanted me to do something for him.

He raised his eyes and stared at me. And smiled, his expression cold steel. Then he held out his hand, the three vials glinting, the black sludgy liquid inside gleaming, unmoving. For a moment, I was afraid to take them. The thought of touching Nathaniel's skin made me want to shudder. But I controlled myself and reached for them. They were the key to freeing Samantha.

That was all the incentive I needed.

But I needn't have worried about touching Nathaniel. When I reached out, he held them out so I had to cup my palm to receive them. He dropped the vials into my hand and moved back. Seemed he also had issues with touching me.

Feeling's mutual, you bastard.

I gripped the tubes in my hand, a shiver running up and down my spine. I held dark magic in the palm of my hand, dark magic created with my own blood. Nathaniel's voice broke through my thoughts. "I have given you three. You should only need one to destroy the circle, but I have given you more just in case."

I nodded. I was grateful he had thought of it, but I wasn't about to bow to him in gratitude. "Anything else I should know?" He frowned. "Like how I'm supposed to use this in the first place?"

I had no idea if I was supposed to smear the substance on me or the floor or if I was supposed to drink the damned thing. Did Nathaniel really think I knew? Or was he playing with me, wanting me to ask questions every step of the way?

He cleared his throat, giving me a thin smile. "Drop the blood on the outer circle and allow it to penetrate the magic until the ward is broken. The magic will not harm you, whether you are inside or outside the circle. Whatever you are planning to do, just be quick about it."

"Why? Does the power of the magic fade?"

"No. Of course not." Nathaniel's jaw hardened and he drew both his hands into tight fists. Someone was sensitive. "I was only advising you to get in and out as fast as possible. People who would use dark magic to cast a spell like you described will not take it lightly when they sense their ward is broken."

"How will they sense it?" I asked, frowning.

Nathaniel smiled. "Are you not able to sense any attempt at penetrating a ward set for you? Perhaps one set for your vehicle or your home?" His tone was so suggestive I did a double take. Did he somehow know my home was warded? He chuckled, picking up a decanter half filled with an orange liquid. He swirled the liquid around and studied it as it spun. "What did you think, Ms. Morgan? That I wouldn't know that the chances are very high that someone in your profession would ensure she is protected while she sleeps?"

I scanned his face, my gut saying he knew more than he was telling me. He knew about my ability to jump, so it stood to reason he'd had me checked out. Or maybe he'd tried to enter my home and found out the hard way it was warded. Natasha's protection wards packed a punch. I hid a smile and decided from his tone it was most likely the latter. "Anything else?" I asked, eager to get going.

He shook his head. "You have everything you need. And don't take too long or I may get bored and decide to play break the statue and stick it back together."

From the gleam in his eye I suspected that was exactly what he would do. When he waved at the door, I moved to leave, then twisted to look at Drake still hovering a good five feet off the ground.

How do you say goodbye to a man turned to stone? I stared at him, trying to tell him "I'm sorry" with my eyes. Trying to assure him I would be back for him as soon as physically possible.

Then I turned and hurried to the door without giving Nathaniel a backward glance.

CHAPTER 17

MEL

I tugged open the car door and dropped into the driver's seat, turning my purple stone around in my hand. I'd seen it sitting on the bottom stair where Drake had left it. Slipping the chain over my neck, I centered the stone on my chest and patted it, blinking away the tears that burned behind my eyes.

All my emotions were rising to the surface, bubbling over now that I was out of Nathaniel's house. I shuddered and slammed my fists into the steering wheel. I didn't care that it hurt, didn't care that it wouldn't help any.

I just hit it as hard as I could as hot tears filled my eyes and overflowed. I'd gotten Drake into this situation, and now I'd left him there at the mercy of the necromancer he'd warned me not to visit. Would he ever forgive me? I sniffed, wiping the tears away with the back of my hand. I guess I would have to save his ass to find out. I would be happy to face the music then.

Right now, I had to get moving and bring Samantha home.

I started the car and drove off down Nathaniel's drive, spitting gravel as I went. The sound of it spurred my anger at the sorcerer for holding Drake ransom. I'd walked right into a trap, only Nathaniel hadn't even known I was coming.

I sped home, not caring a hoot for speed limits, my mind focused on Drake and on dark magic.

AFTER TAKING a long shower that failed to remove the traces of Nathaniel's vileness, I set about packing my bag for my trip to the demon plane. I planned to get some rest and then be on my way.

Now that I had the spell, I didn't have a single reason to waste any more time. And with Drake waiting, I had all the more reason to hurry. Bag packed, I switched off all the lights and was about to head upstairs when a loud explosion rocked the wards around the house.

I probed the magical protection, just the way Natasha had taught me, and found a spot that must have been weakened by the explosion. With the darkness for cover, I went to the windows and peered through a crack in the drapes.

The windows looked out onto a small grassy lawn that was currently overtaken by a variety of weeds. And was also currently occupied by a body.

I gasped as I recognized the familiar curve of a cheekbone and the shock of inky black hair.

Saleem.

I glanced up and down the street and found it surprisingly clear—nobody drawing their weapons, nobody running away from the scene. Saleem remained unmoving on the grass and I made the decision on the fly.

No way was I going to leave him lying there. What if he was dead? I shuddered as I unlocked the door and raced down the steps. I scrambled across the grass and fell to my knees at his side. He was completely still and didn't appear to be breathing.

I touched the side of his face and cupped his cheek. His

stubble prickled against my skin and shivers of heat ran through me. I let go and sat back.

What the hell was going on with me?

The man could be dead and I was all hot for him? Shaking those thoughts out of my head, I scanned Saleem's body again. I lifted his chin and bent close to his mouth, hoping to feel the warmth of air on my cheek or to hear the soft sound of breath to confirm he still lived.

Nothing.

For a moment, I wondered if mouth-to-mouth would work on an unconscious djinn, then dismissed the idea. I needed to get him inside. The street remained dark, and no neighbors' curtains twitched. I decided to take the chance.

I grabbed hold of him and jumped straight into my sitting room. Leaving him on the floor, I went to close the front door, quickly rechecking the ward. It was thin where it had been damaged but still strong enough to prevent penetration. When I returned to the room, I came to a shocked standstill. Saleem was sitting upright where I'd left him, a dazed look in his eyes. He studied the room as if he was wondering how he got there.

When I entered, he stared at me, shocked. "You jumped me?" he asked, his eyes wide with disbelief.

I nodded, then smiled. "Well, depends on what you mean."

He gave a rueful grin and rubbed his head. "As much as I would have liked you to jump my bones, I think we both know that's not happening. At least not tonight."

I folded my arms and raised an eyebrow at him. "Yes, I jumped. I had to. Your life was in danger. Or rather, it appeared your life was in danger." He seemed to be feeling much better for someone who appeared dead only moments ago. "What the hell happened to you?"

He shrugged, giving me a grin that looked a little too sheepish for my liking. "I had a bit of an accident."

"Accident?" I frowned, then remembered the explosion and the damage to my wards. "Did you try to penetrate my wards?"

"Unfortunately, yes. Guilty as charged." He heaved himself up to his feet and dusted himself off. What? Did he think my house was dirty or something? I gritted my teeth but could not force myself to be angry with him.

"So what the hell is it that you want? And why is Fulbright trying to enter my home without my permission?"

"Fulbright is not involved."

"Oh, so it's *you* who wanted to enter my property without a warrant?"

"I don't need a warrant."

"What?"

He held out his hands and grinned. "No, what I meant was I'm not here on official police business. I came to ask you for your help."

"And I'm supposed to swallow that story?" I glared at him, furious with him, but my breath hitched as I studied his sexy grin and his long locks. Man, was he too good-looking for my health.

He shrugged. "I'm being honest with you. I need your help. That's the beginning and the end of it."

"What does your detective friend think of this?"

Saleem shook his head. His jaw tightened and his eyes hardened to black coals. "Fulbright knows nothing of my decision to speak to you."

So, the djinn was not a fan of his partner. "So what are you doing with him anyway?"

"Omega had him on its radar for delving too close to paranormal business. He's asked one too many wrong questions. They think he is too much of a loose cannon, and someone up there probably got tired of him investigating you. Now that he has his attention on Samuel, this thing will only escalate. So I am here to keep an eye on him."

I snorted. "So Omega is covering its ass?"

He nodded. "That's part of it. There is something going on with all these recent disappearances. And they were clear that it's not anything to do with you. It's Fulbright who's causing a stir; that's what's got Omega in a shitstorm."

I considered what Saleem had just said. So Omega had its eye on Fulbright. I made a mental note to get Steph to dig up a little bit more information on Omega's interest in the kidnappings.

For now, my gaze narrowed on the djinn's face. "So what do you want with me?" I asked, and then flushed when his eyebrows raised and his lips curved into a sexy grin.

Looks like I had to watch what I said in front of Saleem. All my words seem to have alternative connotations. And as much as I liked what I saw, the last thing I wanted to do was encourage him. I folded my arms and waited, keeping my expression cool as I stared at him.

He scratched the back of his head. "I'm here because I'm looking for someone. And I need your help to find her."

Her? My first thought was *who was this woman?* And who was she to Saleem? Annoyed, I tried to tamp down the twinge of jealousy that rose within me. I had no right to be jealous. He wasn't even anyone I knew. One conversation does not a relationship make. Add that to the fact he was Omega, and it meant I should stay far, far away from him.

I hesitated. Clearly, he needed my help to find someone. I wasn't in the habit of saying no to people who needed my help. "Okay, I would need some details. Who is the missing person? Where was she last seen? How long has she been gone?" Saleem's features relaxed and he looked relieved. "I have to warn you, I'm on a case right now. So, although I am happy to help, you'll have to wait until after I am done with this job."

He nodded. "Of course, I understand that. She's been gone so long. I suppose one more day, or even one more week, wouldn't make much of a difference."

His face darkened and took on an expression of such sadness

that I felt tears burn at the back of my eyes. I wanted to comfort him, but I didn't move. I just waited for him to speak, giving him all the time he needed.

He took a deep breath and continued, "My mother disappeared two years ago. It's not something that makes any sense. She had a lot of responsibilities. So it's not as if she would have just up and left. Omega looked into it for me, but came up with nothing. In all the time that I've been working for Omega, they have been searching for my mother. And still they haven't found her."

I raised my eyebrows. So *this* was what he wanted to talk about. "Are they sending out the right people to look for her?"

"I'm not sure what they've been doing. Every time I ask them, they assure me they are doing the best they can to find her."

"It's not as if Omega doesn't have the best resources for finding a missing person," I said, still unsure how to make him feel better. "Maybe they're just not looking in the right places. Or maybe whoever has her has outsmarted them so far."

"That's what I was thinking," said Saleem. "And that was the reason I decided to come to you. The timing seemed to have been perfect. So when this job came up, I put my hand up for it."

I frowned. "How did you know that I would be able to help you"?

He chuckled. "You have a certain reputation, Ms. Morgan. Most people at Omega know exactly who you are and what your success rate is for finding missing people."

"Really?" I asked, slightly impressed that I seemed to have made a name for myself. There was no denying that I was proud of my track record. Could this have been the reason for Omega's investigations into missing persons? Were they investigating me?

"Yeah, and you're not only known for your track record. Everybody knows that nobody messes with Tracker Morgan."

I was even more impressed. "Now tell me a little bit more about your mother. What were her habits? Was there anyone she could have pissed off? Was she involved with anyone the least bit shady?" Saleem frowned. "Please don't be offended. I just have to ask all possible questions and look at it from all possible angles." I waved a hand at my sofa and Saleem sat, although he didn't look too comfortable.

He leaned forward, resting his elbows on his knees and linking his fingers. Long, elegant fingers that made me think naughty thoughts. I really had to get a grip. I forced myself to listen to what he was saying. "I completely understand, and I guess for you to do your job properly you need to know everything. I have to confess I don't really want to tell you the whole truth about my mother, but I feel I can trust you. And if it can help you find her, then it would be worth it."

I sat on the sofa opposite him and digested his words. He seemed so serious, his eyes dark, his lips a thin line. "It is possible there is one good reason why someone would want to abduct my mother. You see, my mother is Aisha, Queen of the Djinn."

I swallowed a gasp. I blinked and tried to process the reality of who I actually had in my home. Saleem was a prince. Something inside me reminded me that he was not only a prince, but a demon prince, which put him securely on the don't-even-think-about-it list.

CHAPTER 18

MEL

Saleem chuckled. "Lost for words, are you?" he asked, his eyes gleaming with amusement.

I nodded. "Definitely lost for words. It's not often that my home is graced with the presence of a prince."

He shrugged. "Well, in the last two years, the last thing I have felt was princely." He shook his head. "Believe me. Sometimes I think it would be much better to not have the burden of my name weighing me down."

"So who is looking after your kingdom now that your mother hasn't been around?"

"That would be my brother," he said, his face a little sad. "He is too young to bear the responsibility of the kingdom. But we had no choice. I was the only one who could go looking for Mother. I do go home often enough to help him out. He's getting the hang of it."

"Does he not like the job?"

"Not really. He's more of a free spirit. Responsibilities weigh him down. Stifle him. I just hope we can find our mother. At least get some resolution as soon as possible. I'm just not sure how long he will put up with the responsibilities of her kingdom."

"So tell me, why is it *you* were the one to join Omega? I'm assuming you joined as a way to take advantage of Omega's resources?"

Saleem nodded and rubbed his forehead. "All elder djinn sons are trained for war. Riz was not destined for the throne. A bit of a slacker, really." He grinned. "And he'll tell you himself I am right. He just wasn't leader material and Mother knew it. Harsh as it may sound, Mother wrote him off as a potential for the crown."

"So *you* are the rightful king?" I swallowed, feeling a little shell-shocked.

"Yeah, for what it's worth. All I'm doing now is treading water, waiting to hear something about my mother's whereabouts. I've wasted two years with Omega, and I figure it wouldn't hurt to get some help."

I sat forward. "I'll help you. I have somewhere else to be tomorrow. But as soon as I get back, I promise I will give it my utmost attention."

Saleem rubbed his hands up and down his thighs. I dragged my eyes away from them and took a deep breath. "About your fee?" Saleem spoke, bringing my attention back to him. "How much do you charge?"

I stared at him, for a moment unsure what to say. Do you offer to work for royalty for free? But most royals were loaded, so they would be able to afford to pay for my services. And yet the thought of taking money from Saleem made me slightly ill. "Look, let's leave the money talk for after I find your mother."

Saleem gave me an odd look, but just nodded. Then he rose so suddenly I was immediately wary. "Okay. Thanks for taking my case." He stood there looking so uncomfortable and out of place. Gone was cocky, sexy Saleem.

The man before me revealed a vulnerability in his eyes that made me want to walk over and give him a hug. People lose people all the time. But people don't just disappear—they leave, they break your heart, they betray you. Disappearing is endless.

No closure until someone leads you to a grave or a dumpsite in a hillside a hundred miles away.

I stood up and walked around the coffee table. I wasn't sure what to do with my hands. Suddenly I was self-conscious and uncertain. Usually I was hard and unemotional so the families wouldn't use me as a crutch. So I could walk away if I failed. But with Saleem, I wanted to rush off right this minute to find his mother for him. I knew his pain. Knew it so well I breathed that agony day and night.

"I know it sounds trite, but don't worry. I'll find her if she's—" I clamped my mouth shut.

Put a foot in it, why don't you!

But he didn't take offense. Just rubbed his face and gave me an awkward grin. "If she is alive. I know. You don't need to soften the reality of it for me."

I placed my hand on his and tried to ignore the sizzle of heat that ran through my fingers. "I do think there is more value in her alive. So I'm pretty confident she is alive." I was so tempted to ask him for something of hers, so motivated to do a projection right now. His eyes were my undoing—filled with gratitude and yet still containing a playful spark. I sighed and I made up my mind at that moment. "Do you have something of your mother's?"

"Yeah. Some clothes. A set of jewelry."

"Anything biological?" He frowned. "Hair. Blood. Something living that contains her DNA. It's the most accurate way of tracking her. The DNA will lead me right to her."

Saleem remained silent for a few moments. "Yeah. I do have something. A silver brush and comb set. Omega asked specifically for her hair so they could sample her DNA in case it could help them find her."

I snorted. "What were they expecting to do with it?"

"They said a DNA profile on file would be advantageous.

DNA from certain investigations could then be compared to hers. They did say it was a long shot."

"How soon can you get me the hair sample?" I asked. Saleem held up a finger, and before I could tell him to drop it off with Steph the next day, he disappeared in a flash of fiery red and orange embers.

I stared around the room, my mouth still hanging open. Just as I clamped it shut, Saleem reappeared, giving off a blast of fiery sparks. He held out a small felt covered box, the center of its lid inscribed with a golden crest. "No time like the present."

He seemed pretty proud of himself, eager to give me what I needed. I didn't have the heart to tell him to wait so I leaned forward and took the box, careful to ensure our skin did not touch. I needed a clear head and he seemed to understand.

He stepped away and walked to the sofa. I moved to the coffee table and sat opposite him again. Placing the box on the table, I opened the lid and laid it aside carefully. The crest looked beautiful and fragile.

Don't break it, Mel.

I lifted the silver hairbrush from the box and sure enough, dozens of strands of jet-black hair still clung to the bristles. I glanced up at Saleem. "Can you take a strand out for me and place it on the table?" His eyebrows fluttered in question. "I don't want to touch it until I'm ready." He nodded and proceeded to remove a strand and place it beside the box. Then he sat back and waited.

I shook my hands and took a deep breath. Then I reached out and picked up the strand, holding it carefully between two fingers. The feedback was strong and my gut tightened, the strength of the resonance pressed me hard into the back of the sofa. I glanced up at Saleem, who'd moved to the edge of his seat, his face twisted with concern.

I gave him an encouraging smile. The strength of the feedback meant nothing yet. Until I tested it, it remained merely a strand of live DNA. I swallowed and sat back. Only when I was settled did I allow myself to test the thread properly, and my mind went flying along the link.

And touched life.

The beats of a heart echoed back to me, soft sighs of breath. I felt tension and frustration creep toward me through the connection.

Then I let go of the connection and leaned forward to place the hair on the table.

Saleem cleared his throat. "Is she–"

I raised a hand and he stopped speaking. "She is alive. And it feels like she is well. I didn't sense pain. But I did get a strong impression of anger and frustration. So your mom is certainly not happy about her situation."

He laughed. "Yeah. Mother isn't the kind of woman who happily sits back and lets things happen. She's a doer and she's pretty feisty."

I nodded and smiled. "I get the feeling she wouldn't be giving her captors an easy time."

"Nope." He grinned at me, but there was a hardness around his eyes that spoke of years of worry and grief. "Thanks for doing that for me. Knowing she is alive and well is enough to tide me over until you complete your case."

I stood up and tightened the muscles in my legs. They threatened to fall from beneath me. I must have been far more tired than I realized. Projecting was exhausting, but not to such an extent that a short test would drain my strength this way. It meant I needed a solid rest before I left to fetch Samantha.

Saleem spoke before I could. "Is there anything I can do to help you?" When I frowned in confusion, he continued, "In your case, I mean."

I shook my head. Although I was down one with Drake out of commission, I preferred not to get Saleem involved in my work, especially with his double whammy of Fulbright and Omega.

"Thanks for the offer, but I'll be fine. I'll contact you as soon as I have my stuff done." Then I turned and walked to entrance hall, and was relieved when he followed me. Before I opened the door, I asked, "Are you okay though? Not feeling dizzy or anything?"

"Me? No. I'm fine." He laughed. "Oh, you mean after my fainting spell? Yeah, I'm all good. That's some powerful magic you have there. I'll sleep peacefully from now on knowing you are well-protected."

"Who do I need protecting from?" I asked, then blushed at the heated look he gave me. For a moment, I couldn't remember to breathe. He didn't answer. Just opened my front door and ran down the stairs and across the lawn to the undercover vehicle at the curb.

He waved as he drove off and I shut the door, feeling suddenly bereft. Even the room felt empty without his presence. I shrugged the thought out of my head, locked up, and headed for bed.

CHAPTER 19

I rose early, dressing in dark blue jeans and a white peasant blouse, the purple stone sitting comfortably on my chest. I threw on my favorite leather jacket, needing it more for the convenience of its pockets than anything else.

Scooping the three vials of black liquid out of my jacket pocket, I placed them on my dresser and brushed out my waist length hair. I threaded a piece of cord through the loops on two of the vials, then as I braided my hair, I wove each of them tightly into it. I secured the braid then tucked each bottle into the folds of the weave so well nobody would ever know they were there. I slung the final vial around my neck and it lay low on my chest alongside Natasha's protection spell.

Gathering up my bag as I went, I hurried to pop my head into Steph's room. The door was open and I gave it a knock, leaning against the doorjamb. Steph looked up from the small desk we had installed in her room for her homework. She was odd in that she preferred to keep her schoolwork far away from her tech stuff.

"You ready to go?" she asked, looking at me over the tops of her glasses. Her hair was thrown into an untidy bun at the back of her head and held in place with a nicely sharpened pencil. When I nodded, she said, "Be careful, okay?"

"Aren't I always?" I raised an eyebrow.

"No. You're not." Her eyes narrowed at me.

I grinned. Didn't have a worthy response. "Don't trash the place while I'm gone."

"Damn. To think I had a day of trashing all planned." Steph made a disappointed face. As I moved to leave, she said, "Hey, where's Drake? I haven't seen him since yesterday."

I hesitated, then turned back to face her. When she saw the look on my face, she gasped, her face growing pale. "No. What happened?"

"Nathaniel has him. He's holding him hostage until I get him a portal key."

"A portal key? You mean a jump-to-a-different-dimension kind of portal key?" Her mouth dropped open. Then she shook her head. "But that would be a bad idea. A key in the hands of a sorcerer like him?"

"Yeah. I'm with you on that. Only thing is it's the key for Drake's life. No choice, really." I shrugged. "I'll go for it once I get Samantha safely home."

Steph gave a slight shake of her head but I could tell she was still in shock. I wanted to comfort her but the thought itself made me feel too vulnerable. As if sharing my fear for Drake would unleash the floodgates. I smiled weakly and turned to leave. Steph sat there in silence.

I loped down the stairs to the kitchen, glad to be away from Steph's far too perceptive eyes. After a quick breakfast of toast and coffee, I was ready to leave. I flipped open Samantha's file and grabbed the plastic packet holding her tooth. I tugged my bag over my neck and slung it across my body.

Just being careful, in case I had a hard landing. Taking a deep breath, I picked up the packet and slit the top open, then tipped the tooth into my palm. I felt the immediate connection to the child, the steady thump-thump of her heart, and a sense of sadness that would have brought tears to my eyes if I hadn't hardened myself to my emotions.

Every time I went on a rescue mission, I deliberately tamped down my emotional response. Often, I had no idea what I would see when I arrived on a jump. If the person was dying or dead, the last thing I needed was to be bawling my eyes out. I needed to filter my emotions, keep them under control.

Now, I refused to feel the echo of sadness in my own heart. I concentrated on the feedback, grabbing hold of the ethereal link shimmering between Samantha and me. I slid along the thread, allowing myself to go careening along so fast I hit ether in under five seconds. I was more confident with this projection, only because I'd done it before. The only precaution I was taking was to project first, rather than jump right into Dastra.

Catching my breath, I slid through the ether, ignoring the insistent tugging of the energy waves. At last, I reached the Veil and sighed. The ether taxed my strength with the sensory overload. I transitioned through the Veil and appeared in Samantha's cell.

Silence weighed down on the iron room and I blinked in the dull light of the single fluorescent bulb in the center of the ceiling. Movement on the cot bed drew my eyes to the shape beneath the rough spun blanket. The little girl sat up and rubbed her eyes as she stared at me.

A glance around the room confirmed it was safe. I jumped, my physical body following the thread linking itself to my spirit in Dastra.

I rushed to the edge of the pentagram. "Are you okay?" I asked her, wanting to jump the ward, grab her and get her out of there.

She nodded, her lips curving into a cute toothless grin. "I knew you would come back for me."

I smiled. "I always keep my promises," I said, giving her a little wink.

"I know." Her words were solemn, and I did a double-take. She was so serious, as if she really did know me. What other powers did this kid have? "Okay, Samantha. Can you tell me if the guards come in to check on you regularly?"

"I think so."

"When was the last time?"

"Some time ago." She shrugged but the smile she gave me was encouraging. "But it's okay. I can tell when they are coming." She tilted her head to one side for a moment, as if listening to a faraway sound I couldn't hear. "They plan on checking on me but not for a while yet. I will tell you if anyone is coming."

I nodded slowly. "So you can just read their minds?"

"Yup."

"And they haven't tried to block you?"

"Nope. Only the Cloaked Man is hard to read. It's all a bit fuzzy when I sense him around. And that's not supposed to happen." The little girl frowned. She was clearly unhappy at her apparent ineptitude.

I only wasted a moment wondering who the Cloaked Man was. Then I grabbed the vial from my neck and began to unscrew the lid. "Since we are all clear for now, let's get this show on the road." I knelt at the edge of the magic circle, which buzzed with energy and stank of dead meat.

"What are you doing?" Samantha asked. She craned her head to see, while swinging her legs back and forth.

"I have a spell that will help me break this ward." I tipped the contents of the tiny bottle onto the ground allowing it to cover the edge of the circle at my feet. The line was thick but there was enough blood to coat the breadth of it.

The black liquid mingled with the bloody substance of the ward and sizzled and boiled. I held my breath and waited as the energy rose, as if the ward knew it was being penetrated. Then the hum of magic faded away, leaving a simple pentagram drawn on the stone floor. Nathaniel's charm had worked.

Although I knew the ward was broken, I wasn't planning on going rushing in. I reached a toe out and touched the outer circle, knowing if the ward had held, it would send me flying through the air like a magical electric shock.

Nothing happened.

I stepped into the inner circle of the pattern, my feet smudging the lines of the pentagram at the center. Still nothing happened and I finally let out the stale breath. Spurred into action at the confirmation of the broken ward, I rushed forward and grabbed Samantha, still swaddled in the coarse blanket. She linked her small hands around my neck and smiled at me.

As I strode out of the circle with her, she said, "Thank you, Miss Morgan."

Just before I jumped, I said, "My pleasure, Miss Cross. Now hold on tight and don't let go."

CHAPTER 20

MEL

I landed in my kitchen, arms wrapped tightly around Samantha. She looked up at me, her eyes large and round and entirely unafraid. She smiled and her face lit up. My heart clenched. What an adorable kid. But I had no time to fall in love with kids.

A friend's life needed saving. Stat.

Setting her on the ground, I yelled for Steph. The gray blanket slipped off her shoulders to reveal her stained and rumpled clothing. I frowned. "When was the last time you had a bath, young lady?"

She scrunched her forehead, then shook her head. "Can't remember. I think it was a long time ago."

"Yeah," I said, waving my hand in front of my nose. "You stink."

Samantha giggled, her eyes lighting up again. She glanced at the doorway as Steph came barreling into the room. My geek friend skidded to a halt before us. She smiled at our visitor and said, "Now who is this cute little thing?"

I introduced the two and glanced at Steph. "Can you go grab Samantha some clothes from the store? I'll take her upstairs and get her all cleaned up." Then I looked at Samantha and wrinkled my nose. "She smells." That brought on a fit of giggles and I held my hand out to her.

Metal tinkled as Steph grabbed her keys from the bowl on the kitchen counter. "I'll go over to Catherine's Kids and get her a few things."

I nodded, then flicked my eyebrows at my bag. "Take my card."

I headed up the stairs as Steph rummaged in my bag. The door slammed seconds later, just as we entered the large airy bathroom. Samantha let go of my hand and stared up at the ceiling, then spun around. "Wow, this is a ginormous bathroom."

"It is." I nodded seriously, then turned my attention to the huge claw-footed tub. "Tub's huge too."

She squealed and ran to the tub, leaning over into it. "Wow. It's so big." Her words echoed inside the empty tub, setting her off into another fit of giggles.

"Yeah, it needs a whole lot of water. You want to turn the taps on and start filling it? I'll just grab you a towel." I handed her a bottle of bubble bath.

She bobbed her head and leaned over, twisting the taps open and humming as she poured the soap into the running water. As I fetched the towel, I wondered at her resilience. She'd been kidnapped and kept in a cell for months, yet her personality still made it through. Strong kid.

Back in the bathroom, we waited, splashing at the water as it filled, steam rising and filling the room. "Right, let's get these stinky things off."

Samantha toed off her sneakers, then leaned against the tub to remove her socks. She wrinkled her nose and held it away with two fingers before dropping it onto the shoes. I smiled. She was so cute. The other sock gone, she dragged off her shirt and flung it onto the growing pile. I examined her body as she removed the rest of her clothing. My greatest worry was that her abductors had beaten or abused her or worse, but she looked fine—no physical damage that I could see.

I knew I had to ask the hard questions soon, but I wanted to wait until she was more comfortable.

Samantha climbed over the edge of the tub and sat into the water with a plunk. She giggled as clumps of foam rose around her neck. Soon she was content to play with the clouds of bubbles.

"How are you feeling, honey?"

She turned her gaze to me. "I am fine, Miss Morgan. And you don't have to worry about me. Those horrible people didn't do anything to me. They wanted me safe and alive so I could be trained to do what they wanted." I did a double-take, shocked at the mature, serious way she spoke. I'd totally forgotten she could read minds.

Score one for the kid.

"That's good then." I hesitated as I poured shampoo into my palm. I spread it on her head and began to scrub as I asked, "Do you have any idea what it I'm me to a party soon. A big party. They said they wanted me to listen to a few people and tell them what those people were thinking."at

"Any idea where this party was or who they wanted you to listen to?" I asked, then instructed her to rinse.

She held on to the sides of the tub and bent her head back, dipping it into the water. I scrubbed her hair, rinsing off the soap. When she sat up, she said, "No. They never mentioned any names to me." Her mouth turned down. "They treated me like a kid."

I hid a smile. "That's not very nice of them. Especially since they wanted you to do stuff for them." Samantha nodded and her expression cleared. "Right, as soon as Steph gets back with those clothes, we can get you dressed and call your dad to come fetch you."

"My dad?"

My stomach twisted at her oddly sad expression. "Yes, honey, your dad sent me to find you."

She shook her head, her eyes filling with tears. "But my daddy is dead. They told me so."

"No, honey. He is very much alive and he asked me to find you and bring you home." I reached out and stroked her now pink cheek. "Those people were evil. They probably wanted to convince you he was dead so you wouldn't think of home."

She nodded, then made large circles in the water, tracing deep valleys in the piles of bubbles. She was about to speak when we heard the front door slam again. "That would be Steph with your clothes." I handed her a sponge and a bar of blue soap. "Here, scrub up. The water's getting cold."

She obeyed and I went to the door to wait for Steph. She strode down the passage, a pretty pink and cream striped bag in her hand. She handed me the card. "Jen refused to take it once I explained who the clothing was for."

I smiled and pocketed my card. "Leave it in the spare room. And Steph, thanks."

"Hey, I loved it. Haven't shopped for little girl's clothes since . . . . Well since I was a little girl." She giggled, and it was infectious.

I'm I returned to the tub, grabbing the large bath towel. "Right, Stinky. Out you get." She giggled again and stood up, water draining off her reddened skin. I wrapped her in the towel and carried her out of the tub, setting her down on the lush mat. As I rubbed her dry from head to toe, I sniffed at her cheek. "Okay, maybe I can't call you stinky anymore. You smell like roses."

Her grin was wide, revealing her toothless gums. She submitted to the drying then pulled the towel around her as I stood and led her to the room. Steph had laid out a pair of pink jeans patterned with multi-colored glittery splashes. Beside it was a hot pink belt and an equally hot pink t-shirt with the words "Too Kewl for Skewl" on the front. Underwear, socks, headbands and a brush were piled beside it.

"Wow," Samantha squealed with delight and ran to the bed. Then she turned to me. "Thank you," she said shyly.

"My pleasure, Samantha." And it really was a pleasure to see this kid so ecstatic. "You get changed and I will ring your dad. I have to go out for a while, but Steph will get you something to eat." She nodded and I left her to change, heading downstairs. I fished my phone out of my pocket and dialed Martin Cross's number.

He didn't greet me. His first words were, "Have you found her?" His voice was breathless and pained, as if afraid to hear my answer.

I kept my tone neutral. "Yes. I have her with me. You can fetch her as soon as you are able. She's at my place." I gave him the address.

"How is she? Is she okay? Is she hurt?" The questions came barreling out.

"She's fine, Mr. Cross. I've given her a bath and a change of clothes. She's about to get something to eat. She's okay. Doesn't seem traumatized. But I do want to talk to you when you get here. I'm heading out for a short while but I should be back in a couple of hours. Could you stick around until I get home?"

He sounded hesitant, but said, "Sure. I'll be there in half an hour, depending on traffic. I'll see you when you get home." He rang off, probably thinking I wanted to talk to him about the balance of the fee owed on completion of the job. Didn't matter to me. As long as I got him here I was happy. I was curious if he knew anything at all about his daughter's abilities.

My next call was to Chloe but it went straight to voice message. I sent her a text confirming Samantha was with me and could she come as soon as possible. I wanted Chloe here when I told Cross his daughter was a paranormal. She knew how to calm the nerves.

And from past experience I knew there would be plenty of nerves needing calming.

CHAPTER 21

MEL

I headed to my office to grab some supplies. Once I got to the DeathTalker's estate, I would need a distraction in case the High Priestess's library was occupied. Thanks to Drake, we were well-stocked with small explosives and smoke bombs. I could blast a hole through a wall if I wanted to. Just hoped I wouldn't need to.

Concentrating on the DeathTalker's estate, I jumped to the grounds a few miles outside of Chicago. I'd considered the best place to jump and figured I was better off arriving among the trees that surrounded the property. Hidden behind a stand of oaks and elms, I readied myself to project into the house.

I'd been there before to discuss Veil transitioning with the last High Priestess. Kira, the current High Priestess, I didn't know, so I wasn't about to knock and ask for an appointment.

A magical ward pulsed around the mansion, not unlike the one protecting my own house. Only this one was strong and powerful, and laced with dark magic. They would have to use dark power, considering the type of people who would want to get in.

Like Nathaniel.

I snorted softly and wondered how I was supposed to get past the ward. Light magic wards were easy for me to break through, but dark power was a whole other ballgame. I was stuck on the outside until I could find a way in that didn't include exploding myself while breaking through a dark magic ward.

I blinked, a vision of my blood dripping into a bowl appearing before my eyes. Dark magic was just what I had with me. In two little vials still tied in my hair. Would it work? And how would I use it to begin with? I had no time to go seeking advice.

I needed to get this done fast and get back home to speak to Cross about his child. For now, I would just have to guess. For a physically drawn spell, I had to remove the drawing. What would I need to do for an ethereal spell like this one?

I removed one of the tubes and held it up in the light. Maybe it was enough to just hold it in my hand and walk through. The spell still had power so I hoped it worked. Circling the property, I looked for a way to get closer to the house that would provide sufficient cover. Just ahead was a line of hedges that ran along a path toward the building. Where it ended at the edge of a stone-floored patio, a row of enormous potted trees took over. I scrambled along the hedges, duck-walking most of the way.

As I reached the patio, I began to feel the energy of the ward strengthen. The difference was the dense darkness seemed to want to swallow me whole. I struggled to breathe, then tried to calm myself down. I had no choice. I had to get in or I might as well say goodbye to Drake.

Not going to happen.

Creeping closer to the ward, I gripped the vial in my palm. My hand shook as I extended it, my fingers almost touching the magical shield.

Then I stopped.

What if it wasn't enough? For the demon's spell, I had to pour the blood onto the markings on the floor. Maybe the blood itself needed to go through first. And I didn't exactly have the means to throw drops of the blood onto the ward. I considered breaking the bottle but wasn't confident it wouldn't just shatter into a dozen unusable pieces. The best way was for the blood to be on my body to allow me to pass through. On my skin.

I unscrewed the lid of the bottle and poured some of the blood onto my forefinger until it was coated in the black sludge. I sealed the vial using my other fingers, sticking the pointer digit out, hoping not to drip blood all over myself. Tucking the vial into my jacket pocket, I inched closer to the ward. The energy pulsed, the hair on my cheeks picking up the almost nonexistent movement.

Using my forefinger, I probed for the ward and felt the resistance when my blood-drenched digit touched it. It had the bounce of an invisible balloon but softer, giving off a hum only a few people could feel. I pressed harder and my finger popped through the shield. I winced, expecting the doors to the house to fly open, spilling DeathTalkers all intent on finding who had penetrated their wards.

But nothing happened.

My finger was now on the other side of the shield. I sighed with relief and said a silent prayer as the rest of my hand followed. Still nothing happened. No magical shockwave sent me flying backward. No ethereal alarms were set off. Or at least none I could hear. I relaxed and followed my hand through the ward and onto the patio. Clear of the magical wall, I ran to the end of the patio and ducked down beside another large potted tree.

I leaned against the warm stone wall and concentrated on projecting into Kira's library. Floor-to-ceiling windows let the daylight into the room and I held my breath in the brightness. The library was still and silent. I was about to jump fully when

Kira moved from a shadowy corner and walked into the center of the room, holding open a large book and staring hard at its pages.

Damn. Not what I'd hoped for.

Her attention remained on the book and she seemed not to know I was there. Now I had to find a way to get her out of the room or I was stuck outside without the key. I moved from the library, slid through the wall into the passageway and scanned the ceiling for smoke detectors.

Smoke would do to set the detectors off. And I had come prepared.

I floated along the passage, then poked my head into the next room. More smoke detectors dotted the paneled ceiling of a large sitting room filled with overstuffed chairs that were threadbare, and looked like sitting on them would be dangerous to the chair's health. The room was close enough and looked like it would serve my purpose.

Without hesitating, I followed my projection and jumped to the center of the room. A glance around me revealed a large glass-fronted cabinet beside the door. Sufficient space to hide on the far side of it. But if the last searchers were too diligent, they would walk in and see me. I couldn't take that chance. Large purple drapes framed the windows, heavy brocade patterned with garish gold fleur-de-lis. I'd have to make do with hiding behind the hanging fabric.

Rummaging inside my bag, I withdrew two smoke bombs. Then I set the timers for thirty seconds and jumped to the reception hall at the front door. I set one bomb under a gigantic round table bedecked with an arrangement of dry flowers. It sat in the center of the hall and would serve my purpose perfectly. I scanned the hall to ensure it was clear and hurried to set the bomb beside the large triple footed base of the table. Then I jumped straight back into the room beside Kira's library.

I dropped another bomb beside a sofa, hidden from the doorway, then scurried behind the drapes. From where I hid, I could see the mirror above the ornate stone fireplace. It reflected the doorway, allowing me to see who came and went. I made it just in time.

The timer coughed and with a soft puff, smoke hissed from the contraption, slowly filling the room. I waited for the alarm to kick in, holding my breath from both expectation and the need not to breathe in too much of the smoke. The formula would make my eyes sting and tear and irritate my throat until I coughed continuously.

Seconds later the alarm blared, hurting my ears as the wail rose and fell around the building. A door opened nearby and fabric swished as Kira hurried into the sitting room. I watched her reflection in the mirror as she scanned the room then turned to hurry down the passage. Moments later, I heard her voice echo toward me.

"Move. We need to get outside fast." Her voice rang cold and unemotional, unperturbed by the possibility of this beautiful building burning up around her.

Satisfied they were gone, I jumped straight into the library. Once I got my footing, I hurried to a low cupboard on the left of the room. The last time I'd been to this library I'd wanted a portal key to make my life easier. My jumps had always been taxing on my strength, and my first year had been peppered with nose-bleeds, extreme dizziness and blinding headaches when I did multiple jumps in a day. Even now, I kept my jumping for emergencies.

I opened the cupboard and found shelves filled with metal keys, all blank and waiting to be programmed to individual users. Talia, the last High Priestess, had summoned a junior to assist, and the younger DeathTalker had fetched a blank key from this very cupboard. Only in the end, Talia had refused my request when she learned I already had the ability to move through the Veil on my own.

Her advice was to practice and become stronger and to leave

the portal keys to those not blessed with my ability. I sniffed at the memory as I pulled out three keys and tucked them into my bag. Then I jumped straight to Nathaniel's front porch and sighed with relief.

Drake was almost free.

CHAPTER 22

MEL

I slammed the garish bronze knocker on the door, watching as the lion's head bounced off the dark wood. The door swished open and Nathaniel's corpse-like butler stared at me, eyes cold black chips. "The Master awaits you downstairs." Then he moved aside for me to enter. As soon I stepped over the threshold, he shut the door and stalked off.

Raising an eyebrow, I followed as he led me to the stairs to the necromancer's underground lair. The butler halted at the top of the stairs then bowed and left me there, disappearing down the hall in shadowy silence. My heart thumped as I hurried down the stairs. The door was shut and I swallowed, praying Drake and I would get out of here fast. I pounded on the door and waited, feeling the cold of the underground stone seep into my bones.

The door opened fast enough and Nathaniel stood there, a satisfied smile on his face. He waved me inside and I walked to his desk, slinging my bag forward to withdraw the blank keys. Over in the far corner stood Drake, a perfectly carved statue watching in stony silence.

Not long now, Drake.

I dropped the metal disks on the table and they clanged together, the musical sound ringing around the stone room.

"Ah, well done, Ms. Morgan." Nathaniel clapped his hands together and hurried to the desk. He stood close to me as he reached for the keys, so close I could have easily stabbed him in the gut. But that would be a mistake. I hardly knew if Nathaniel was strong enough to regenerate himself. I could just be killing myself by trying to end his sorry life.

I took a step back and waited as he examined the disks. "Are you satisfied?"

He nodded but his attention remained on the keys.

"You have what you want. Now let Drake go."

His eyes drifted to me, lips curling into a cold smile. "Did you think it would be that easy?"

Icy dread filtered through me. Nathaniel was going to cheat me. I gritted my teeth. "We had a deal. Do you plan to dishonor that deal?" He stared at me as if considering how best to answer my question. "It's not hard, Nathaniel. Yes or no." I shifted a little to face him head-on. "But before you speak, let me remind you that I am not a meek little human bowing at your powerful feet. If you renege on this deal, I can promise you I will not be quiet about it."

His face darkened, his jaw a granite curve. He gripped the keys in tight, white fingers and I wondered if he was stupid enough to try to break the deal. The glare he sent me had shivers running up and down my spine. He knew he would have to kill me to ensure his dishonor wasn't revealed.

"Oh and don't think you can just kill me and be done with it. A number of people already know I am here; they also know what you did to Drake and what you made me do to save him. They will not be inclined to keep quiet should I conveniently disappear while visiting you."

I watched as he stewed on my words, his eyes darkening. He

glanced over at Drake, then back at me and shrugged. "You are no good to me dead," was all he said.

I frowned. Heaven knew what he meant by that, but I certainly didn't want to stick around to find out. I walked to Drake and looked at Nathaniel over my shoulder. "Release him." Not a request, although I wasn't quite sure what I would do if he didn't free Drake. The hum around me reminded me his lair was protected by a powerful spell, so jumping was not an option.

A moment went by in which I glared at Nathaniel. And then he flicked his hand at Drake. I spun back to Drake and watched, holding my breath. The stony solidity eased, the gray color lightening.

His skin scrunched as he moved his facial muscles. I met his gaze and let go of my breath. Drake stared back at me, relief so evident in the glossiness of his eyes. He blinked slowly. I stepped closer in case he fell forward, watching as his color gradually returned. But he didn't move.

Soon he looked like Drake again, no longer giving me that stony hard-faced gargoyle stare. He frowned and glanced down at his body, tilting his head. He tried to move but it seemed his body hadn't received the message yet. I looked over at Nathaniel, who stood watching, his fingers tracing the keys unconsciously. He paid no attention to me, his gaze remaining on Drake.

When I turned my attention back to Drake, I sighed with relief. He was moving his shoulders, struggling against the hold the spell had on him. At last, he stepped forward and sagged against me.

"Here, put your arm around me," I said, struggling under the gargoyle's weight. He was so heavy I strained to support him and was very near collapsing beneath him. He seemed to understand, throwing his arm over my shoulder and taking more of his weight onto his legs. I glanced over at Nathaniel, who had lost interest in my reanimated friend and was back at his desk, caressing his keys. "Let's get you home," I said as I guided him to the door.

"Wait," Drake said, stopping our progress.

"What?" I met his gaze. Seeing the fury in his eyes, I shook my head. "No. We have no time. And he is too powerful."

"The bastard turned me to fucking stone." He gritted his teeth, his jaw pumping with anger.

"And he will turn you to fucking stone again if we don't get the hell out of here now," I growled softly, not even daring to check on Nathaniel. Knowing how quietly he moved, chances were he was right behind us.

I tugged Drake forward and expelled a sigh of relief when he grunted and let me lead him to the entrance. As I pulled open the door, I glanced at Nathaniel whose face was dark, his eyebrows looming over shadowed eyes.

He nodded at me and a shiver ran up my spine. Maybe it was the smug smile on his face, but something told me he was not yet done with me.

CHAPTER 23

MEL

I jumped back home as soon as we got to the main floor of Nathaniel's house. I didn't bother to wait until we had left the building. Didn't care if it seemed rude. Besides, I wouldn't have been able to support Drake for much longer. We arrived in the kitchen just in time. Drake pitched over and would have landed on the floor had we not appeared directly in front of the gigantic kitchen table. He fell onto it, gripping the edge to support himself. I pulled a stool over and placed it behind him, and he slowly sank into it, relief shining on his face.

"You okay?" He nodded at my question, giving me a wry grin. "So you can say 'I told you so' any time you want," I offered, a sheepish smile turning up my lips.

He shook his head and sighed. "No. There's no point. And besides, you got the spell and saved the kid, right?" He stared at me, intent on my answer.

"Of course, I got her," I said, wondering if Cross had arrived yet. I pointed to the ceiling. "She's probably upstairs. And the father should be here by now too."

The doorbell rang, echoing along the passage to the kitchen. I gave Drake a warning look that said stay-where-you-are and headed for the entrance. I flung the door open and Chloe stood on the porch, smiling.

"Hey." We spoke in unison, then laughed. I gave her a quick hug and shut the door. Though not before scanning the street in front of my house. Empty. Good.

I closed the door and waved Chloe into the kitchen. "I think Drake may need you more right now." She raised her eyebrows in question, but with Drake sitting not twelve feet from us, I shook my head, then nodded in his direction. He'd tell her if he wanted to, although he probably knew she'd find out anyway.

As Chloe entered the kitchen, I took the stairs two by two and went in search of Mr. and Miss Cross. I found the little family in the spare bedroom, sprawled on the floor; Martin Cross reading his daughter a story while she lay curled on the carpet, her head on his lap, hugging a multicolored teddy bear close to her chest.

I leaned against the door, and would have left them to it, when Samantha opened her eyes and grinned at me.

"Mel. You're back." She scrambled to her feet and ran to me, throwing her arms around my waist.

I fluffed her curls and said, "You been taking care of your dad?"

She nodded, her blonde ringlets bouncing up and down. Cross met my eyes over her head and gave me a smile so filled with gratitude and emotion that I had to blink away hot tears. He got to his feet, holding the little storybook tight in his hands. "Thank you, Ms. Morgan." His voice broke and he cleared his throat.

I smiled. "It's my job, Mr. Cross. I do the best I can." He nodded, but I wasn't sure he totally understood. This could have gone the wrong way. I could have brought home a body instead of this bouncy little spark of a kid. Maybe he didn't want to think about it. And maybe that was for the best.

I looked down at Samantha and said, "Right, Squirt. I have

someone downstairs I would like you to meet. And I think you will like her very much."

"Is she your friend?" she asked, her forehead scrunched. When I nodded, she said, "Then I think I will like her, too." I laughed and headed out the door.

I wanted to stick my hand out, and knew she would take it and we'd head down the stairs hand-in-hand. But I didn't. I'd already gotten too close, inviting Cross into my home. I'd crossed the line with the Cross family, and it was time to put some distance between us because I certainly wasn't planning on keeping up a relationship with them. I had enough going on in my life. I didn't need to play at being an aunt.

My throat tightened and I cleared it as I reached the ground floor. I didn't look back, just headed straight to the kitchen where Chloe was holding Drake's hands in hers and Drake was looking very uncomfortable.

When he saw me enter, he tried to tug his hands away but Chloe held on tight. I glanced at her, hiding a smile, but when she gave me a wide-eyed innocent look I wanted to laugh. She was enjoying this far too much.

"Okay, Squirt, this is my friend Chloe. She also happens to be a doctor." Samantha stuck out her little hand and Chloe took it, giving the girl a warm smile. "Doc, this is my friend Squirt." Samantha giggled. "Oh, I meant Samantha."

Chloe grinned at her. "So should I call you Squirt or Samantha?"

Samantha laughed. "Samantha. But you can call me Squirt if you like. Mel calls me Stinky," she said, grinning at me.

"Hey, I couldn't help it if you were stinky." I glanced back at her dad, who hovered in the doorway. "Mr. Cross, this is Dr. Chloe Murdoch and my partner Drake Darvon."

Everyone shook hands, then Cross turned to me and said, "I think you can call me Martin. I can't thank you enough for what you did for my family." I nodded, not wanting to get too touchy-feely.

"Okay. Martin it is." I moved toward the doorway and said, "Why don't you guys come to the sitting room and get comfy. The Doc here has a few questions for Samantha."

Everyone filed out of the room and followed me, except for Drake. I hoped he'd relax a bit. I really should have gotten him into bed.

In my front room, I waved them all into seats, and Chloe took my armchair while the Cross family sat on a wider plump sofa. I perched on the sofa near the door. I was planning on leaving the questions to Chloe, but from her expression, she wanted me to start.

I took a breath. "Mr. Cross. Sorry, Martin." He gave me an awkward smile. "You will have to forgive me but I need to ask you what will seem like a very odd question." I waited for him to nod before continuing. "Have you noticed anything strange in the last few months?"

Samantha's head snapped up, her eyes meeting mine. Her face was contorted with worry. I gave a small nod and a quick smile but it didn't seem to make her feel any better.

"I'm not sure what you mean?" Martin said. "Strange?"

"Yes. In your home, with Samantha. Anything."

He shook his head and stared at me, perplexed. A glance at Chloe said I'd done my part and it was over to her.

"Martin, what Mel is trying to ask, without upsetting you, is if you have noticed anything odd or unusual about Samantha." Martin glanced at his daughter who sat beside him, still clutching her colorful bear. Only now she squashed it so hard I was worried it would bust its seams.

"No. There's been nothing strange." He seemed genuinely confused, so I knew Chloe would proceed with caution.

But then Martin yelped and snapped his gaze to his daughter. "What?" He stared at her, so confused it looked like he was about to cry. I glanced at Chloe, who suspected what I did. Samantha was talking to her father in his head. At least he hadn't run screaming from the room.

Yet.

The silence stretched on for a bit until Martin met my gaze, as if he were looking for me to say it was all a joke. I shook my head. "This is real, Martin. Samantha was targeted most probably for her ability. We aren't entirely sure what the abductors were planning, but we do believe it has something to do with supernatural talent." I took a deep breath and forged ahead. Might as well ask the biggie. "Why did your wife leave?"

I deliberately left out the word "you." I didn't want to scrape his wounds raw again. But he shook his head, looked at his child, then back at me. His face held a look of resolution. "Samantha's mother didn't leave us."

I could have cut the silence with a knife. "Where is she?" I asked softly, glancing at the little girl who sat opposite me, completely unperturbed.

"She is in a mental care facility just outside of the city." He turned to Samantha. "I'm so sorry, Sammy, I didn't mean to lie to you. I just didn't want to upset you."

She tilted her head and looked at him with the eyes of an ancient soul. "Don't worry, Daddy, I've known for a long time."

Martin wrapped Samantha in a bear hug, a soft sob escaping his lips. "Why didn't you tell me, honey?"

"I didn't want to upset you. You always got so sad when you thought of Mommy. I didn't want to make you sad."

My throat closed and tears burned my eyes. Chloe's eyes met mine and I could see she was just as affected. Neither of us said anything while Martin absorbed the maturity of his little girl.

When he turned to me he seemed calmer, and I wondered if Chloe had been needed after all. "So, these people that took Samantha. Will they come back for her?"

"There is the possibility they will." His face fell but I wasn't about to sugarcoat the reality. He needed to be strong and hard or Samantha would be left with nothing. "It's why Chloe is here. She will take you to a safe place until your home can be warded."

"Warded?"

"A magical spell to prevent demons or dark creatures from entering your home."

He nodded as if this was all just routine. Only the contained horror in his eyes gave him away. "Can't you catch them?"

"Not yet. We don't know anything much about them. Not enough to know who they are and how they operate. But we will try. I work for an organization that will be sending their operatives out to catch these guys." I stopped speaking. I wasn't going to promise we would catch them because I had no idea if Sentinel or Omega could find them. I hoped so, but I didn't want to make any guarantees. They had been through enough.

"Martin. What was the reason your wife was admitted to the care facility?"

He looked pained. "She heard voices. All the time, everywhere we went. It never stopped. It was driving her insane. She chose to go. Asked to be put into solitary care." As he spoke, his eyes grew larger as he slowly met my gaze. "Do you think she is like Samantha?"

I nodded. "It's very likely that she is." I couldn't bear the guilt I saw in his expression.

I glanced at Chloe, who said, "Don't worry, Martin. I will see about bringing your wife home. All she needs to do is learn a few techniques to control her abilities."

He nodded, the creases of worry and guilt easing a little. "So you don't think there is anything wrong with her?"

Chloe shook her head. "From what I heard about your daughter's abilities, I don't expect anything to be wrong with her mother, but let's keep the final diagnosis for after I have visited her." She got to her feet and said, "I have some arrangements to make. I think it's best you both stay here until I get things organized."

She glanced at me for confirmation and I nodded, turning to Martin and Samantha. "Yeah, make yourselves at home. Chloe won't be too long."

artin headed upstairs to finish reading Samantha her story and I peeped in on Drake. The kitchen was empty. I hoped he'd taken his ass to bed. Fishing in my pocket, I grabbed my phone and sent Saleem a text. With Samantha and Drake both safe and sound I was free to help bring home the Djinn Queen. My phone pinged. Saleem's text said *Knock knock.*

I smiled and went to the door, flushing at his cheeky grin. Man, he was too sexy for my sanity.

For a moment, his features darkened. "You ready?"

I nodded and led him to the living room. "I need to grab my bag, then we can get going." I hesitated for a second, then turned and went out the door, hiding my hot cheeks. I bounded up the stairs, headed to Hacker Central, and I slipped inside as Steph glanced up at me, a smile at the ready.

"I have to go out again. You think you're up for handling Drake and the Cross family?"

"Sure. As long as Drake calls when he needs his diaper changed." She raised an eyebrow. I knew she was annoyed because all this babysitting encroached on her PC time.

"I'm sorry to ask you for this, but if you knew what he went through—"

She folded her arms and leaned back in the seat. "Maybe, tell me?"

I sighed and gave her the brief version, watching as her eyes popped and her face went red as I described what really happened to Drake. "Crap. Okay. No more diaper jokes."

"It wasn't easy seeing him like that."

"Yeah, must've been hard." Steph's eyes widened and she snorted.

I tried to hide my grin. "It wasn't funny." That just made her giggle. "Look after them, you hear?"

Giving her one last warning glare, I hurried to my room and grabbed my bag from beside the door. I peeped into the spare room to see Samantha asleep on her father's arm, with him sitting at an awkward angle, his eyes closed. I left them to sleep and hurried back to Saleem.

When I entered the sitting room, Saleem was on his feet, pacing. "I wasn't gone that long." I grinned.

His eyes lit up as he turned to watch me enter. He shrugged. "Just eager to get going."

I pursed my lips and nodded. "Right then, let's go." When I held out my hand, he took it. The touch of him sent hot shivers up and down my spine. Just the feel of his skin next to mine set my heart racing. I blinked, trying to shake the attraction off. I needed to concentrate.

I still had a connection to his mother, a memory of the threads along which I'd projected to see her the first time. Following the thread, I floated ahead, projecting first, wanting to be careful. I made it all the way back to the room in which Saleem's mother sat.

Her lips were set in a hard, angry line, making the rest of her face an assortment of shadowy slashes. Her high cheekbones and almond eyes screamed her Persian heritage. Beautiful, even as she aged.

And stern. She looked like she was capable of ruling a kingdom.

Happy she was still safe, I returned to my body. Gripping tightly to Saleem's hand, I jumped, landing us among the trees at the edge of the property. Large overhanging branches gave us good cover to observe the grounds of the house and still remain unseen.

"Her room is protected," I said as we studied the house.

"Protected like your house?" he asked, chuckling.

"Yup. Just like my house." I grinned. "So no trying to jump through it."

"Yes, ma'am."

I frowned, scanning his face. "You ready?" He nodded, his eyes roaming the large grounds. Between the wall at the perimeter and the walls of the house stretched a neatly manicured, almost endless lawn. A pathway edged all the way around the house, dotted here and there with gigantic ceramic pots and carefully pruned trees. Whoever had Saleem's mother didn't suffer from lack of money.

An armed guard turned the corner and strode along the path, passing a line of picture windows. He reached the far corner to take the turn and I tugged on Saleem's sleeve. "Let's go. The sooner we get in, the sooner we get your mom out."

He didn't answer, just moved to stand beside me. "The gazebo," he said, then disappeared, leaving behind a fluttering of orange and black embers. A shadow appeared at the far edge of the small structure and I followed, arriving close to him. Too close to him. I couldn't step forward to steady myself. Instinctively, I tried to step back but it was too late. I was already falling. Straight into Saleem's arms.

He grabbed me and held me a little too close to be legal. His face was so near, his mouth mere inches from mine. So close that our breath mingled and all it would take was for me to move slightly forward for our lips to touch. Saleem gazed back at me, eyes heavy-lidded and sultry.

Somewhere on the grounds, gravel skidded and an engine revved. We pulled apart, looking around for the source of the disturbance, but we had entered at the back of the property. The sounds traveled to us from the driveway at the entrance. I blinked and took a deep breath, trying to control the speed of my heart. What the hell was I doing, almost making out with an Omega operative? And while entering a property illegally? We were vulnerable crouching behind the gazebo. I'd never lost sight of the mission before.

I flicked Saleem an annoyed glance but his eyes were already on the building a few feet from us. From our vantage point, we watched another guard take the corner and head along the path toward us. Saleem breathed deeply, so harshly, I asked, "What's wrong?"

He shook his head, his gaze remaining on the approaching man. "The guard. He looks familiar." Saleem met my gaze. "Too familiar."

My phone vibrated in my pocket. I ignored it for now. Frowning, I glanced at Saleem. "What do you mean? You know him?" My voice rose and I had to remind myself to keep it down.

When Saleem nodded, I went cold. "He's Omega."

"Omega took your mother?"

His jaw tightened, tanned skin tense and tight. "Maybe."

I flailed about for a reason. "He could be working for the abductors without Omega knowing," I offered. But the feeling of dread that blanketed me suggested otherwise.

All Saleem said was, "Maybe." A few moments of thick silence passed and then he drew in another harsh breath. "The only way to find out is to find out."

"Right then, let's do this." I put a hand on his arm, hoping to make him feel a little better but knowing it would probably not help at all. The possibility that this was all Omega's doing made my blood boil. And I wanted to know the truth. Now.

"Can you lead us to her?"

I nodded. "But how are we going to penetrate the magic?"

"You said the ward is only around her room?"

"Yes, but it's powerful and dark. I can travel through most wards. It's rare that a ward is too strong for me to penetrate."

"What if we got close enough that she could leave the room herself? On the off chance the ward is meant to keep her in and not prevent her from leaving."

"Why hasn't she just teleported away from them?"

"I've been wondering the same thing all these years. They must have her bound in some way. A powerful curse should do it. The witch who casts the spell needs to be strong. Dark helps."

"Good enough reason to get her out as soon as possible." He nodded, but his thoughts were already on the building.

He got up into a crouch. "Let's go."

We were about to jump when a buzzing sound caught my ear. I held onto Saleem's arm and felt him tense. Tilting my head, I listened, trying to see if I could hear the sound again. It didn't take me long to figure out that I hadn't heard it. I'd *felt* it. Deep in my gut and in my bones. Worse, deep inside my skull. It pulsed and throbbed like a living thing, making me taste bile at the back of my throat.

I dug my fingers into Saleem's arm. "Don't move. There's a ward around the property."

"I thought you said there wasn't."

I gritted my teeth. "So I thought." I shook my head. "This thing is powerful. So strong it makes me want to puke. But it's also spelled to be undetectable from a distance."

"A trap." His words were an angry growl.

"Exactly. And one we almost stepped right into."

"So we can't get inside?"

"Not this time. We need something to break the outside ward

as well as the inner one holding your mom." By now, the guard was too close, so I remained silent as he strode by. Seemed their watch was on a short timer, about three minutes apart.

After he passed and was out of earshot, Saleem said, "I know him as well. He was one of the additional support operatives I had on my last job."

"Then it's probably Omega." I said the words, feeling a sense of dread filter through me. "But why would they want to keep your mother hidden away? How would it benefit them?"

Saleem shrugged. "No idea. It's certainly not because they wanted me as an agent."

"Are you sure? You are quite valuable in the sense that you are the only demon-born that can be trusted, especially with your power to jump."

He frowned and studied my face. "It is possible. The last job I had was to enter the Graylands and try to retrieve a blue stone."

"You mean the stones that control ghosts and spirits?"

He nodded, his eyes guilty. "I didn't enjoy the subterfuge, the lies. I felt like I was betraying a friend the entire time."

My eyes narrowed remembering a very recent case where the sister of Alpha Walker Kailin Odel had been trapped in the Graylands, slowly going mad. "You're talking about the Greer Odel case, aren't you?" He nodded, his brow furrowed. "I did the initial tracking but found her in the dead lands. I have to admit it got me a bit upset knowing what it was doing to her mental state. Did her sister get her out?"

Saleem nodded, his face darkening as he looked back at the house. "Yeah. Kai got her out but Greer is dead."

My eyes went wide but it wasn't the time to go further into how the walker had died. I'd ask him later. Once we were safely home. "Ready to leave? It's pointless sitting here watching the guards circle the house."

He seemed reluctant to go and I understood. "Your mom is okay. She's strong. Besides, we have no way to enter the house.

We could try again. Bring a witch with us to counter the spell and the ward."

Saleem nodded slowly, his eyes still scanning the house. I knew what he was thinking. Any one of those upper floor windows could lead to his mother. It would be incredibly hard to come this close to her then turn back and leave her here. But we had no choice. I placed a hand on Saleem's arm. He patted it. "Yeah, I hear you." Then he sighed and shifted around. "Let's get back."

I nodded and in an instant, we were back in my sitting room. For a moment, I wondered if Saleem would disappear somewhere to nurse his wounds, but he was still at my side, finding his landing feet. We'd arrived so close to each other I could see the golden streaks in his onyx eyes. He stared at me for an awkward moment, our proximity causing a slow heat to rise in the pit of my stomach. Then he turned to leave.

I grabbed his sleeve. "Wait. What are you going to do?" He didn't owe me an explanation but he swiveled around anyway. I didn't move my hand.

"I'm going to do a little investigating of my own." His voice held a steel edge. He tried to soften it with a reassuring smile but it didn't work. There was no reason why he shouldn't be pissed off at Omega.

"Be careful," I said softly, worried for his safety. Omega was not an organization to be messed with.

He moved closer. "I will. I'm just going to be asking questions for now."

"Questions can get you killed." Saleem had moved so close that my voice had lowered to almost a whisper

He placed a finger under my chin and lifted my face to his. "Depends on the questions you ask."

I swallowed hard. "I'm sorry."

"Sorry for what?" His lips were so close.

Clearing my throat, I answered. "I didn't rescue your mom."

He moved his hand, his thumb grazing the side of my lips. "No, but you gave me proof she is alive. And you gave me hope she can be saved." I didn't know what to say to that, especially with the blood rushing in my ears.

Then he kissed me, claiming my mouth, hard and possessive. This was no tentative kiss. It was deep and steamy, no holding back. I lost my footing and stumbled back a few feet. Saleem came with me, moving until I felt the wall behind me. My arms curled around his neck, tightening so he wouldn't be able to stop that incredibly sexy kiss. He had a hand in my hair, pressing me to him. The other slipped around my back and under my shirt. Skin sizzled as he traced his fingers up my bare spine. I shuddered.

My phone vibrated again in my pocket, breaking through my passion-soaked haze. I'd ignored it the first time. I pulled away, my eyes never leaving Saleem's face. He seemed as reluctant as I to stop, but I had to check my messages. I cleared my throat then shifted to reach into my pocket for the phone.

My blood ran cold the moment I saw the message.

Samantha taken Steph hurt come now.

CHAPTER 25

MEL

I shoved my phone in Saleem's hand, no time to relay the message. I ran from the room, checking the kitchen on my way to the stairs.

"Drake?" I yelled for him and heard footsteps slamming the floorboards as he came running.

"What happened?"

"Demons. Two of them. They appeared in the bedroom. Steph was with the kid. She tried to protect her, to stop them from taking her but they hit her. She's hurt, mostly bruises and maybe a broken rib."

I rushed past him, heading to Steph's room. Saleem's footsteps reached the landing, and Drake said, "Who the hell are you?"

"Drake, meet Saleem." I left the gargoyle and the djinn to get better acquainted and entered Steph's room. She lay on the bed facing the door, her face pale, bruised and twisted with pain. I hurried closer and knelt beside her bed. "I said look after the kid, not get beaten to shit."

"My bad," she croaked.

I laughed. "What happened?"

She swallowed. "I was with Samantha. Martin went out for

pizza and I was keeping the kid company. Probably a good thing I was there or we'd never know who took her. There were two of them. Demons, bulky, red-skinned, sharp teeth. I tried to stay in front of her. Screamed for Drake. They pulled me off but I fought them. They swatted me like a fly." She snorted. "Hit me so hard I flew through the air and slammed into the wall. Sorry, Mel, there's a Steph-sized dent in your wall."

I just raised an eyebrow at her comment. The whole thing didn't make sense. "So they knew exactly where she was."

"And they penetrated the wards," said Drake from behind me.

I sat back on my heels looking at Drake, stunned. Of course, they would have had to breach the protection to enter my home. "Yeah, our wards aren't dark magic. Easy enough to break through if you are willing to dabble in evil." I almost laughed at my words. I'd done exactly that, dabbled in evil, to get Samantha safe. It didn't make it right just because I wanted to do good with it. And I saw the look in Drake's eyes. I glanced away and asked, "Where's Martin?"

"In the room. He's taking it pretty bad." When I rose to go to him, Drake placed a hand on my shoulder. "Leave him. You won't make him feel any better no matter what you say."

I didn't like it, but I conceded. For now, I needed to know if Samantha was safe. "Fine. Go and get me something of hers. A hairbrush or a piece of clothing or something. I'll be in the office."

Drake nodded and strode out the door, and I hurried downstairs to my office, Saleem in tow. As we entered the room, I turned to him. "You don't have to stick around. I can handle this."

He folded his arms, bringing his decidedly sexy chest into prominence. "I am not going anywhere. You helped me, and I plan to return the favor."

I hesitated, not wanting to get him involved but the look of hard determination in his eyes made me smile begrudgingly. "Suit yourself."

Then I went to the large armoire set against the left wall and tugged the door open. I stiffened as I took in my stash of weapons and devices, both of the exploding and the non-exploding kind. Saleem was Omega. How did I know he wouldn't rat me out for having such a large and probably illegal stash?

Some of my weapons were from the demon planes, brought home from other missions. I glanced at him over my shoulder and he chuckled. Raising his hands in submission, he said, "Don't worry, I didn't see a thing." I wasn't convinced and my face showed it. "Look, I mean it," he said. "I don't trust Omega right now. And even if I did, I wouldn't tell them anything. You helped me find my mother. That means more to me than I can explain right now."

I flushed. "Okay," I said softly, and returned to the cupboard to grab a few things to stock up my bag.

Drake's footsteps in the hall announced his imminent arrival and I closed the armoire door to see what he'd brought. His face was dark as he handed me the little brush Steph had bought for Samantha. "No clothing. Just this."

It was all I needed. I set my bag on the floor by the door, took the brush and headed to sit in my chair. My body felt heavy, drained from all the jumping. I sat and was about to grab hold of a blonde strand when Drake said, "What the hell is that?" His voice was low and raspy and not happy.

I looked up at him. "What the hell is what?"

He grabbed a tissue from the little box at the edge of my desk and pressed it to my nose. His movement was harsh, not in the least bit tender. But I wasn't hurt. Drake always got mad at me if I didn't take care of myself. I grabbed the tissue and wiped my upper lip. A thin line of blood marked the white tissue. Damn. The jumps were taking a toll on me. Nine so far in the last twenty-four hours. And four carrying a load.

I sniffed and stuffed the tissue in my pocket. When I looked up, two sets of dark eyes stared straight at me: one confused and angry, the other angry and angry. "Come on, Drake. I promise I'm being careful."

He grunted.

"So what's with the blood?" Saleem asked, but when I glanced at him to answer I found he wasn't talking to me. *Really?*

"Her body can't take too many jumps in too short of a time. She needs time to recover."

"She's right here." I waved my hand over the table at them.

"So, she's been overtaxing herself then?"

"Yup," Drake answered, flicking me an annoyed glare.

"Okay, I get it. Take care of yourself. Fine. Can we just get on with finding Samantha?" I snapped at them. "We're wasting precious time."

I didn't wait for their response. Just returned my attention to the brush. I reached out and plucked a strand from the bristles, already preparing myself for the pull of Samantha's feedback thread. A jolt of awareness went through me as I felt her heartbeat, rapid enough that I knew she was terrified. I slid along the connection between us until I reached her. The room was large.

And familiar.

Nathaniel's lair.

I was so furious I wanted to scream. The jolt of anger sent me flying back to my body and I gasped as I opened my eyes. As expected, both men stood in front of me, a little angrier now that I'd left them without so much as a warning.

But the expression on my face gave away my rage. "What happened?" they asked in unison.

"It's Nathaniel," I said, as I rose and hurried to my bag at the door. "We've got to go. Now." I looked around at Saleem.

He nodded and came to me. "I'm taking you this time."

"What?" I frowned for a moment, confused. "Oh, right, djinn, jumper. Okay then. What are you waiting for?" I raised an eyebrow, noticing Drake's expression of relief at Saleem's offer.

Saleem held onto my arm. "So, just think of the place. It will give me direction since I haven't been there before."

I nodded and pictured the stairwell leading to Nathaniel's underground chamber. I didn't want us to be bounced off the ward to heaven-knew-where. We landed safely and I listened for sounds of the butler but the place was silent. I reached out for the ward and frowned. "Weird. The protection is gone." My heart sank as I assumed the worst.

"The only reason he would remove the ward is if there wasn't anything left behind and he wanted us to know it," Saleem spoke my thoughts.

I sped down the stairs and raced into the room, but all I saw was what I had expected. The place was empty. A fresh pentagram was drawn on the rough stone floor, this time in blood that hadn't yet congealed. I shuddered to think of whom the blood belonged to. Scanning the room, I tried to orient myself to where I'd picked up Samantha's location. What had she been seeing when I'd made the connection?

I needed to get to the exact location to get a sense of her feedback. I could still jump to her with the feedback I had of her, but it would be less taxing on my mind if I could add her physical feedback to the residual. The more tangible a link, the stronger the pull to the person, the less my effort had to be.

Holding on to Samantha's feedback, I projected first. Caution often paid off for me and I always felt more confident if I scoped the place out before jumping. The link took me straight to Samantha, and again she was terrified. I felt a sense of déjà vu. The cell was the same one I'd rescued her from not too long ago. I hurried forward, then halted as I sensed a fresh ward around the girl. Samantha sat huddled on the bed, her knees pulled up to her face. I called to her and she looked up, her gaze tracking straight to me.

Are they nearby?

She nodded. *In the next room. Be careful.*

I returned to my body in Nathaniel's lair. Saleem was watching me. "She's okay. I'm going for her. You go back to the house and wait for me." Saleem was about to protest but I didn't wait to hear it. I jumped straight back into Samantha's cell. This time the landing disoriented me a little. The room spun and I lifted my hand to my nose. My fingers came away bloody.

Damn. I didn't have time for this crap.

Wiping the blood off on my jeans, I moved nearer to the ward. I pulled the last vial from my hair, grateful I'd remembered it was there. I repeated the process, pouring the black liquid onto the width of the pentagram circle. I waited while the liquid gurgled, then when I felt I'd left enough time and the spell would be broken, I reached out to test the ward. No sense in setting off the demons' alarms if the spell didn't work.

My finger reached the ward, and a blast of power siphoned through me. The energy bolt flung me backward so hard against the iron wall that all I managed was a soft "Oomph" before everything faded to darkness.

CHAPTER 26

MEL

The first thing I felt was pain spiking up the back of my skull. My eyes opened to thick darkness and I could just make out a low iron ceiling a few feet above me.

I lay flat on my back, my head pillowed by nothing but bare metal flooring. No wonder my brain hurt so savagely.

The full weight of my head lay right on the throbbing pain. I shifted, pushing up slowly to prop myself up on my elbow. I felt the back of my skull, fingers gently searching the skin for the wound.

When I pulled them back, the pads of my fingers were red and the hair near my scalp caked with drying blood.

My heart raced, slamming against my ribs so hard I felt the vibrations in my throat. I forced myself to breathe deeply, to control the air as it flowed in and out of my lungs.

Once a sense of calm descended on me, I considered my position. The spell Nathaniel had given me had backfired. No surprises there.

Assuming Nathaniel himself was involved in Samantha's abduction, he would have ensured my spell would not work now.

I gritted my teeth, annoyed and impatient. I'd walked right into the necromancer's trap.

And now, Samantha was still imprisoned and Saleem had no idea how to get to me. My chances of rescue were slim.

I scanned the cell, rusted iron walls on three sides, the fourth barred by thick metal rods. The energy of a powerful ward sang in my head and I sagged with disappointment.

Of course.

Nathaniel would have known to protect the cell or he would have lost his prisoner in an instant.

But despite the magic, I had to find a way out.

I struggled to my feet, bending over when my head began to spin. I blinked and held on to my knees until the light-headedness passed. I waited a few moments, gathering my energy.

Then, feeling a little better, I straightened. I tasted bile at the back of my throat and swallowed hard. No time for fainting or hurling. I took a deep breath and walked slowly to the bars.

Across the passage was another cell, a mirror of my own, only empty. I glanced up and down the tunnel outside.

Empty.

Frustrated, I grabbed hold of the bars, the need to let out some of my fury stronger than my sense of self. My fingers gripped the metal bars and a rush of electric energy rushed through me.

My muscles spasmed and my jaw clenched so hard I was afraid my teeth would shatter. I wasn't sure if I let go of the bars myself or if the electric shock had thrown me back, but I found myself falling to my knees, shivering as my hands and legs shook like so much jello.

I couldn't hold myself upright. I just tipped over and lay on the metal floor, my body shuddering as the energy dissipated.

The bars had been rigged with high voltage electricity running through them. I shuddered, glad I was still alive and breathing.

But reality did enough to weigh me down.

I was well and truly trapped.

But just because I wasn't able to jump out of the cell didn't mean I couldn't use my other ability.

Projection was by far the most simple and yet the most powerful method to breach any ward. Nothing was impenetrable to the ethereal senses.

I couldn't just set off in search of a particular person like I did with the people I tracked, but I could allow my senses to drift around the area I was in.

Drifting was uncomplicated.

I just relaxed and let my mind wander, searching out other energy patterns in close proximity to me. The corridors around me were empty, but the cells weren't. The occupant one cell over was hunched over. Anger and frustration resonated from him.

You and me both, buddy, you and me both.

Further along, three more cells were occupied by younger children, all asleep. The last cell was filled with movement, the young woman pacing back and forth, the air swirling around her in furious whirlwinds. I left her to it and drifted into an adjoining passage.

After a few failed runs, I doubled back and went the other way, keeping my senses on alert for life signs. It wasn't long before I came to a room that seemed to act as an antechamber to a much larger space.

The doors were left wide open and the hum of a voice filtered to me.

It was reminiscent of an auditorium or a public hall. Inside, dozens of people, all cowled and dressed in dark robes, occupied tight rows of chairs.

The congregation—for that's essentially what it was—sat quietly, looking ahead at the figure on a dais built from the same rusted metal as the rest of the place. I'd floated in during a lull in his speech.

He took a breath and lifted his head and I gasped, the shock of seeing Nathaniel's features below the dark hood sending me flying back to my body.

Damn, that was the second time it had happened. I really needed to practice my control.

As soon as I got distressed in any way, my projected self was always flung straight back into my body. Not that it was a problem. Just inefficient and disconcerting.

I sighed. Now I knew that the abductions pointed at Nathaniel.

CHAPTER 27

SALEEM

Saleem blinked as he reappeared in Nathaniel's lair. When Mel had told him to wait for her at home, he'd gritted his teeth, annoyed she'd jumped even when she was weak, but he'd understood more than she realized.

He'd jumped back to the house and informed an unhappy Drake of what had happened. Drake's silence on the matter only broke an hour later when Mel still hadn't returned.

So Saleem had decided to go back to the sorcerer's lair, hoping to find a way to discover where she'd gone. Saleem's ability to teleport was slightly different from Mel's.

He went wherever he wanted to go as long as he could find the access points in the Veil. What he couldn't do was track a person and follow their energy trail.

Probably why he wasn't a tracker. Saleem snorted then turned to leave when something caught his eye. The pentagram on the floor.

Saleem frowned and edged closer to study the pattern and the offerings. He looked about, scanning the room and then the pentagram.

He frowned. The fastest way out of the room was to teleport.

And when you couldn't jump, there was only one way available—and that was a portal.

He'd gone to the Graylands with Kailin Odel, the panther walker, and she'd needed a portal key to access the Veil. A portal key and dark water. And there wasn't a drop of water around here, let alone dark water.

Saleem stepped closer to the pentagram. Was it a summoning of a portal? Saleem shrugged. The only way to find out was to try it. He took a deep breath and stepped onto the pentagram.

Energy rushed through him from the floor, rising to the stone ceiling. It shimmered and pulsed, bright and white, an opening of the Veil that beckoned him.

Beyond the Veil were Mel and Samantha, both waiting to be saved. Saleem barely hesitated before stepping through the slit in the portal.

He hoped he wasn't stepping directly into a trap, but he figured, *go hard or die trying.*

CHAPTER 28

SALEEM

In a flash of dust and embers, Saleem arrived in what he assumed to be the demon plane. He wasn't entirely certain which part of Dastra it was, but he felt the hum of demon energy in his bones.

A fitting reminder of exactly what he was.

A demon. Nothing more and nothing less.

His mind went immediately to Mel, and it was as if the mere thought of her enforced a level of calm that he sorely needed. He needed Mel more, but for now he had to get his thoughts together, to concentrate on what he had to do next. He stood at the dead end of a long passage, the weight of the iron walls looming above him.

He hurried down the corridor, treading softly to ensure his footsteps didn't echo. At last, he reached another passage and he slowed before he reached the corner.

He was about to pop his head around it to check if the coast was clear when a pair of Lamia demons appeared almost from nowhere. Their gray-white skin glistened even in the weak light.

Saleem got the barest glance at sharp shiny yellow teeth before he jumped to the end of the corridor, as far away from the demon pair as he could. He'd be screwed if they were headed down his way.

He waited a few moments and when no footsteps pounded the floor toward him, he let out a sigh of relief and returned to the corner.

Mel's face hovered in front of his eyes and he hoped she was okay. Just as he made to take the turn, a voice rang in his head.

Are you a friend of Miss Morgan's? The sweet voice echoed in his ears.

He frowned and looked around him, trying to locate the source of the voice. Had someone crept up on him without him realizing? Or was the speaker here with him but just invisible?

No. I am not invisible. I can just hear your thoughts, even though you are not with me. I heard you think of Mel. Are you her friend? This time the girl's voice was more insistent. Saleem tilted his head and frowned. This kid knew Mel? Then he whispered, "Samantha?"

Yes. That's my name. And you don't need to speak. I can sense your thoughts. You are thinking of Miss Morgan. So you must be her friend.

How do you know I'm not her enemy or maybe one of the bad guys? Saleem asked.

'Cos I saw you thinking about kissing her and I know her. She wouldn't be kissing one of the bad guys.

Saleem almost choked. Good thing he hadn't been thinking of more than just kissing.

Then I would have stayed out of your mind. It would be rude to intrude on adult stuff.

Saleem chuckled. *Are you really six years old?*

I am. Honest.

Saleem grinned. *Do you know where Mel is?*

I think so. You have to hurry. They've taken her.

Did you see her?

Yes. She came to free me, but the magic was too powerful and it threw her into the wall and she fell down. I thought she was dead but I can still hear her thoughts. I was about to talk to her when I heard you think of her. Can you save her?

I can do my best, Samantha. Now can you tell me where she is?

I can't tell you exactly, but I can guide you to her.

Okay then, lead on.

Samantha whispered directions in his ear and soon he was on his way. *How do you know if I'm going in the right direction?*

I can sense you and Mel. And I can feel when you get closer to her. It's like playing Hot and Cold.

What's Hot and Cold? Saleem asked.

It's a game my dad plays with me. He would hide a bar of chocolate and make me look for it. And every time I took a step he would say hot if I was closer and cold if I was moving away from it.

He heard the giggle in her voice and smiled. *Interesting game.*

Saleem hurried to the end of the passage he was following and paused again at the corner. *Don't worry,* Samantha said. *It's clear. Most of the guards are at the meeting with the scary man.*

What scary man?

The one who does the magic. The man who made them take me from my daddy. They want me to do things for them.

Like what?

Turn left and keep along the passage, you're almost there. Samantha paused. *They said they wanted me to go to a big party with the hooded man. They wanted me to listen to someone's thoughts and tell them everything.*

Did they say who the person was?

No. Oh, you are almost there. Turn left again. Oh, be careful, there's a guard coming.

Saleem grabbed his weapon, slipping the safety off with a flick of his thumb. The demon took the turn up ahead and spotted him immediately.

He reached for the walkie-talkie attached to his belt but Saleem didn't give him a chance to lift it to his mouth. The djinn aimed and fired in one smooth move.

The weapon clicked, making a small popping sound that had always made his brother call it the Fart Machine. The djinn were adept at manufacturing weapons, and had perfected the art of making demon-killing guns and ammo.

The bullet hit the demon in the middle of the forehead, Saleem's aim being extraordinarily accurate, one hundred percent of the time. The demon tipped backward and fell heavily to the ground, his walkie-talkie falling at his side with a soft thud.

You are safe now.

Thank you, Samantha. Saleem turned back and hurried to the tunnel the girl had said led to Mel. For an instant, he wondered if this was all a setup and the girl worked for Nathaniel.

If I told you I'm not working for this Nathaniel man, would you believe me? Saleem hesitated. *That's okay. I do understand. You can't trust everyone just because they ask you to.* Before Saleem could think of how to answer her, she said, *You're almost there.*

Barred cells flanked Saleem as he walked along the passage. He scanned each cell as he passed until he looked into the one that contained the tracker. She paced up and down the cell. She hadn't seen him yet and he waited for her to turn back toward him.

CHAPTER 29

MEL

The first thing I said to Saleem was "Don't touch the bars."

Of course, I wanted to thank him for coming. I even wanted to tell him I'd never been happier to see anyone in my life.

Or that all I wanted to do right now was to kiss him senseless because he actually came to save me.

But the moment was gone. Saleem dropped his hands. "The bars have some kind of electrical current running through them. It could kill you."

He shrugged, his lips turning up into a sexy grin. "A bit of electricity wouldn't hurt me."

I raised an eyebrow. "Good to know." When he only smiled wider, I shook my head. "How do you plan on getting me out? Electrified bars, and the cell is warded so be careful about that too."

Saleem's face darkened, his forehead scrunching into a bunch of thin lines. "Well, it looks like we will have to resort to a little kaboom."

"That could work." An explosive force was capable of creating a rip in the ward, a small opening that lasted mere seconds.

I'd have to waste no time jumping through it. I used explosives only as a last resort, especially when extracting those I tracked. The last thing I wanted was for the captors to have immediate awareness of my rescue.

Jump signatures could be followed by another jumper or by someone who had powerful magic. And though I was adept at covering my own tracks, the person I carried usually wasn't.

But now, the situation called for drastic measures. Then I thought of my bag of weapons and contraptions. "But I don't have my bag with me. It's in Samantha's cell. Nathaniel probably has it." My voice was bitter as I recalled the necromancer's face beneath his hood.

"That's no problem. I tend to carry around my own firepower too. I've come prepared."

He dug into his pockets and withdrew half a dozen of Drake's mini-bombs.

When my eyebrows bobbed in question, he said, "When I left your house to look for you, I thought it best I was prepared."

"Smart."

"I know."

"Get over yourself. Get me out of here first, then we can give you the Smartest Djinn in the Room award."

"I see being confined to a cell does nothing for your sense of humor, Ms. Morgan." He winked and moved away from the cell.

But before he could take a step, I said, "Wait."

"Make up your mind, Mel. Wanna go free or not?"

"No, it's not that." I pointed down the row of cells. "There are kids in these cells."

"They won't get hurt."

"They may not get hurt but they may get left behind when we make the headlong dash to leave."

Saleem nodded. "You want me to take them away first?"

"Please. The blast will bring the guards. It's probably better for the kids to be gone when they do get here."

"Okay. Hang tight. I'll be back."

As he moved away, I called out, "Watch out for electrified bars."

I went to the far end of the cell to give myself a better view of the passage and of Saleem. I could only see one cell from my position. Saleem moved toward it.

"How do I know if there aren't any wards protecting the cells?" he asked.

"There probably aren't any. Too many spells to cast and keep going. If they wanted to protect all the cells they would have set one large ward. I'm betting mine is the only one powered by dark magic."

"Okay. It's your head if I end up dead."

"Mmmh," was all I said as I leaned against the wall to watch. He hesitated only a moment before jumping into the cell. After a few long moments of pained silence, he called out. "One down."

I couldn't see what he was doing but I assumed he was teleporting all the kids to my house. I worried that it wasn't protected enough. I hadn't had the chance to get Natasha to come over and strengthen our wards. Just one more thing to do when I got back.

Five minutes later, Saleem strolled up to the bars of my cell, the smile on his face decidedly smug. "All done."

"That fast?"

"Only takes a moment to flash in and flash out." He brandished the little bomb. "Ready?"

"Yup. And remember, I will jump us to Samantha as soon as I'm out." He didn't look like he liked it but he had no choice. I was the only one who knew exactly where she was and we were in too much of a hurry for him to follow my thoughts and jump us.

I stepped back to the far wall and waited as Saleem set the timer and placed the small bomb beneath the bars of my cell. He moved away and five seconds went by.

Five seconds that felt like an eternity.

The ground shook when the explosives were detonated; metal pieces fell to the floor, some missing me by inches.

When I looked up, I made out the mangled mess of the bars lost in a cloud of dust. The dust did nothing to hide the shimmering dome that protected the cell.

The bomb had blasted a portion of the ward open and I ran straight through it and out of the cell to Saleem. I jumped him to Samantha's room so fast he barely had time to look up.

⌇

THE MOMENT we landed in Samantha's cell, I caught sight of the little girl, her arms tight around her brightly colored bear. She grinned when she saw me, clearly happy to see me.

I smiled back at her, then glanced at Saleem. "Hand me a bomb. There's no time to be subtle. We'll just have to take our chances if they follow us." Saleem handed me one of the devices without question.

I hurried to the edge of the ward, using my senses to detect the perimeter of the magical barrier, and placed the bomb on the floor as close to it as I dared.

"Samantha, honey. Can you move back as far as possible?" The little girl nodded, her eyes wide. "Don't worry. Nothing will happen to you. I just want you to be extra careful."

The girl scurried to the furthest end of her cell and squeezed the bear harder.

I set the timer and moved back as far as I was able. Saleem slid in front of me, the breadth of his body enough protection from any kind of detonation.

I wasn't sure if I felt annoyed or grateful for his gallantry. But I remained behind him nonetheless. A few seconds later, the bomb exploded, sending vibrations through the small room.

The full power of the explosion hit Saleem and me, slamming

us into the wall. My head took the brunt of the blow and a moist warmth bloomed at the back of my skull.

I really had to stop smashing my head into walls.

My ears were ringing as the blast subsided. Saleem grasped my shoulders and helped me get back on my feet. My head was still spinning, and I needed a moment to get the room to stop turning.

I leaned on him, taking advantage of his strength and support. Steady at last, the first thing I wanted to know was if Samantha was okay.

I glanced over Saleem's shoulder and sighed with relief. Samantha still stood with her back against the wall, watching the room in silence.

Happy she was safe, I scanned the ward to see if the bomb had worked. And it had. The explosion had ripped a small opening in the magical protection. There wasn't much time before it closed, especially considering how powerful this particular ward was.

"Samantha, can you run to me quickly? Please." I spoke with an urgency the child undoubtedly felt. She did as I asked and ran to me, slipping straight through the rip in the protective wall.

She clung to me and I stroked the top of her head. We really didn't have time for hugs and kisses, but I let her have a moment, however short it was.

"Come now." I patted her shoulder and she looked up at me, her eyes filled with trust. "We have to get going. The sooner we get out of here, the sooner you will be safe."

But we didn't get to do much more than blink. The iron door to the cell slammed open, bouncing against the wall, the harsh ringing echoing around the room.

Two men rushed into the cell: one a menacing-looking red-faced demon carrying an equally menacing-looking ax, and the other hooded, cowled and tall.

I pushed Samantha behind me, and whispered to Saleem, "Take her away but not to the house. Then get everyone out of my place to somewhere safe." Saleem hesitated. "Go now. There's no time. You have to trust me."

I didn't need to look at Saleem to know he would be frustrated and angry. But Samantha had to be saved. So he had to leave.

The air shifted behind me as Saleem jumped, taking our little mind-reader with him. A weight lifted off me.

Knowing that she was safe freed me to do what I needed. Behind me, Saleem's jump signature let off a simmering energy.

I grabbed onto it, a mental lasso, tying myself tight to it. I let the feel of it sink into my mind while keeping an eye on the two men closing the distance between us.

"Don't move," growled the hideous demon.

I would have replied to him, but my attention was solely on the cowled figure.

For a moment, I thought it was Nathaniel coming to confront me. But something told me it wasn't him.

And when the man moved his hands upward, my heart stuttered. He pushed the hood back off his head and met my eyes.

Samuel.

CHAPTER 30

MEL

I blinked, not trusting my eyes, not daring to believe who stood before me. Tears singed my eyes and I blinked them away.

I couldn't allow myself to cry but somehow, that was the only reaction that made sense. Before me—solid, healthy, real—stood Samuel.

He turned to the guard next to him. "Leave us."

The demon stared at him, shocked, "But the Master—"

"I know what the Master said. Give me five minutes and then you can return." Samuel's tone was hard.

The demon didn't move. "The Master said she must be taken alive."

"Don't worry, I don't plan to harm her. I just have a few questions for her."

The demon looked at Samuel, then turned his glare to me. He seemed confused by the unusual request, torn between his master's instructions and the more immediate danger of disobeying Samuel.

In the end, Samuel won.

The demon gave him a hard stare before turning on his heel

and stalking out the room. He didn't bother to close or lock the door.

A message to Samuel; he wasn't going to get complete privacy for his questions. But Samuel wasn't going to leave anything to chance.

He followed the demon toward the doorway, grasped the metal handle on the rusted door and slowly pushed it shut. The only concession he gave was to refrain from locking the door.

He returned to me, but I couldn't wait. I had to know. "So this is where you've been all this time." I was unable to hold back the hurt and the accusation from my tone.

"Yes, Mel." His eyes held a world of pain all of his own. "I'm sorry that I couldn't tell you where I'd gone, or even why. It happened so fast. And then I was here and I couldn't leave without abandoning her."

"How are you even here?" I asked, walking toward him.

I placed a hand on his chest and a bolt of shock ran through me. He was as solid as I was. Solid and real.

But I knew it was impossible. Samuel was still sitting in the chair in his room back home, barely sentient.

He smiled. The curve of his lips benevolent and slightly secretive. "Oh, don't worry. When I get back, there is something interesting I have to teach you."

"You figured out a way to project and still be solid?" I asked, still slightly weak with shock.

In all the time I'd been projecting, I'd never even imagined the possibility of being able to project and be solid. It meant you had to physically be in two places at the same time, solid and real in two places.

As far as I knew, that was unthinkable.

"Believe me when I say that it was not intentional. Like you, I never dreamed it would be possible, but I suppose if one is determined enough, then things become attainable that would have never been so before."

I frowned. He was being so cryptic. "So what exactly are you doing here in Dastra? You do realize we've been worried about your health for so long. Dr. Harper was very concerned on his last visit. Your body isn't in its best condition, you know."

Samuel shook his head. "I have to admit it is a concern, but what I am doing here is far more important than the condition of my physical self." He sounded so haughty I wanted to hit him.

Instead, I folded my arms and glared at him. "That's a bit selfish, you know. People have been waiting and hoping you would come back for so long that very soon they will start giving up on you. Think about your family, Samuel." His face remained rigid. "What's so goddamned important that you need to be here anyway?" I asked, determined to get an answer.

But he just shook his head. "I can't tell you. Not right now." I opened my mouth to speak but he raised his hand. "Someday you will understand. In the meantime, you just have to trust me."

I wanted to rail at him. Tell him he was being stupid. Stupid and reckless and irresponsible. But something in his tone made me stop.

He had a reason for being here. A reason he was not prepared to share with me. A bubble of anger rose within me.

But I knew that once Samuel said he wasn't ready to share, he wouldn't. I'd be wasting my time demanding an answer. And he was right. I would just have to trust him.

For now, I needed to know more about Nathaniel's involvement.

"If you can't tell me what you're doing here, the least you can do is tell me what Nathaniel is up to. He's the one behind all the abductions, isn't he?" I tilted my chin, looking up at Samuel, daring him not to answer.

Samuel nodded. "Yes, the necromancer is the one responsible for the most recent abductions. He's been handpicking young people with particular powers that he thinks he can hold to serve his own purposes."

I frowned. "Samantha said that he had wanted her to attend a party, to listen to the thoughts of the guests. Do you know anything about it?"

"Yes, it's a charity benefit with the mayor as the guest of honor. Nathaniel wants information he can use to coerce the mayor into doing what he wants."

"So you're telling me that Nathaniel has a political agenda." I scoffed, unable to believe the sorcerer would want to play such a dangerous game.

Samuel nodded, his face dark. "Political agenda, and so much more."

"So why aren't you doing anything to stop him?" I asked, challenging him.

"Because that's not the reason that I'm here. I do what I can to thwart his plans, but I can't do anything that will jeopardize my position here."

Before I could ask him any more questions, I was distracted by the sound of bootsteps filtering in from the passage outside.

The door swung open, and slammed against the wall for the second time. I winced, the noise hurting my ears as it echoed through the room.

Too late to ask Samuel any more questions.

I glanced at him to say goodbye, and the expression on his face stopped me. He whispered, "Don't worry now. I will stay as long as she needs me."

I frowned at Samuel. More cryptic. But I didn't have any more time left to ask him what he meant. The guards were almost onto us and if I wanted to leave, I had to go now. I mouthed a silent goodbye to my old friend and jumped from the room.

I used Saleem's jump signature and followed it, almost all the way to his destination. Before I ended up landing right where Saleem arrived, I turned and veered off, using my own power, my mind concentrating on the concrete high-rise that was more glass than any other substance.

I ARRIVED at the entrance of Omega headquarters with the two demons close on my tail. The thought of their bright angry eyes and sharp flashing teeth sent shivers up and down my spine.

I bent forward slightly to regain my balance, my head spinning as if I'd lost a lot of blood. I frowned and pressed my temples.

What the hell was wrong with me? Pain spiked through my head, and I bent over, almost losing my balance when fat drops of blood splattered the bright white marble tiles.

I put a hand to my nose and gasped at the amount of blood that smeared it. Whatever was happening to me, I didn't have the time to figure it out.

I gathered what energy I had left and ran to the armed guard at the reception desk. Tim Rogan knew me well enough that he hadn't taken me out the moment I appeared.

Rogan opened his mouth, probably to ask me what was wrong but then he glanced up behind me. His eyes widened and his hands went to his gun.

I looked over my shoulder to see the pair of hideous demons appear and solidify a few feet from me. A heavy ax came zooming at me and I ducked, feeling my head spin again.

No time for weakness.

The guard beside me dodged a flying dagger and when I looked back at the demons, they seemed to be drawing more weapons out of thin air.

The thought that mere demons were now able to follow my jump signature was too terrifying to contemplate. Was Nathaniel teaching them? Or just lending his power to his guards?

I drew my gun, aimed, and fired. Rogan did the same. Bullets flew at the two demons and for a moment they seemed immune.

Our ammunition seemed to bounce off them. *Damn.* They must have had some kind of protective force around them. But protective fields like that never lasted very long. Not unless you were creating your own field.

And very few demons possessed the power of magic. I continued firing, and knew I would have to reload in a moment.

Just when I thought my luck was up, the taller, redder and grosser of the two made a sound like he was punched in the gut.

Good.

I hoped I'd hit him.

My demon gun was loaded with some pretty powerful bullets. They were filled with poison that would fell even the biggest demons, bullets fashioned to explode once they entered the flesh, spewing out their poisons faster and more efficiently, delivering death on a silver platter.

The demon tilted forward and fell on his face so hard he smashed the tiles beneath him, the force sending ripples of cracks, and displaced tiles outward from his body.

My gun clicked, announcing the empty chamber, but I didn't bother to reload. The second demon stiffened, the middle of his forehead blooming black where Rogan's bullet had entered.

"Superb shot," I said.

He grinned and holstered his weapon. A rush of footsteps around us announced the entry of Omega's onsite operatives, but they'd missed the party.

Relieved, adrenaline dispersing from my veins, I felt my body weaken. The room spun and I sagged, and would have fallen had Rogan not caught me.

He laid me on the floor, shucking out of his jacket. He rolled it up and placed it under my head, for which I was extremely grateful. My head wound was still throbbing like hell.

"Are you hit?" His eyes and voice exuded concern as he scanned my body for bullet wounds or bloodstains.

I struggled to get a word out, then just shook my head. It hurt, but moving a body part was easier than speaking.

Around me, the noise level increased as agents shouted for

assistance, cleanup, and whatever else was needed to fix the fact demons had entered Omega's super-protected facility. Darkness encroached at the edges of my vision and I almost succumbed when I heard a familiar voice.

"Mel. Mel, are you okay?" Saleem's sexy tones penetrated my haze and I blinked.

I wanted to just relax and give myself over to the pull of sleep, but I needed to see his face more.

I struggled to lift my lids, eventually managing to crack them open a little. He hovered close, his smile comforting, his dark hair grazing his cheek as he bent over me. I gave him a poor excuse for a smile.

"Hey." I swallowed, the single word so hard to emit.

"Hey, yourself. Welcome back."

The smile never left his lips, but it didn't reach his eyes either. Worry shadowed his face as he gazed down at me.

"Was I out?"

"For a few seconds. Never a dull moment with you around is there, Tracker?"

"Nope. I need to get back on my feet. Fulbright must be wondering where I am."

Saleem snorted. "He sure is. About to blow a gasket so you better haul ass and annoy him some more."

I laughed but the sound came out more like a choked cough. Darkness threatened again but I held it back. "How's Samantha?"

"Safe."

"And the rest?"

"Also safe."

"Get Natasha to strengthen the wards." I managed to get the words out, although it seemed to be getting harder and harder.

"Already done."

Emotion welled inside me and hot tears singed my eyes. It felt so good to be taken care of. Especially by Saleem.

"Be careful. I might decide to keep you around," I said, my voice husky.

Saleem laughed and began wiping the blood from my upper lip and nose. "Let's get you cleaned up and checked out. Drake was right, you never listen."

I wanted to respond, to laugh it off and say I knew what I was doing. But my head was spinning and my limbs were heavy and I was so, so tired. I'd done what I needed to do.

Samantha and the other kids were rescued. And the best part was I knew Samuel was safe and well.

Although I still wasn't sure who he was looking after in Dastra. When he'd had his moment of lucidity and said *she needs me*, I'd thought he was referring to Samantha. But clearly it wasn't the little girl, as she'd been rescued. So who could she be?

My heart tightened. Could Samuel be keeping an eye on Ari? But before I could think about it further, the darkness encroached, thick and suffocating.

The last thing I heard was Samuel's words:

"Don't worry, Mel. I will stay as long as she needs me."

~ TO BE CONTINUED ~

Thank you for reading. The SOULTRACKER Series continues with Demon Kin.

ACKNOWLEDGMENTS

To Inklings and the Indie Inked ladies- You Rock!

Thank you to my editor Tracy Riva and my proofreaders Karen Mead & Jenn Waterman, for helping to make BLOOD MAGIC shine.

To DH & Daughters: hasn't this been an awesome journey?

To Kate Strawbridge- cover artist and the best friend a girl could ask for. You have magic fingers and magic eyes!
And to my readers. Don't stop reading. . .

ABOUT THE AUTHOR

I have been a writer from the time I was old enough to recognize that reading was a doorway into my imagination. Poetry was my first foray into the art of the written word. Books were my best friends, my escape, my haven. I am essentially a recluse but this part of my personality is impossible to practice given I have two teenage daughters, who are actually my friends, my tea-makers, my confidantes… I am blessed with a husband who has left me for golf. It's a fair trade as I have left him for writing. We are both passionate supporters of each other's loves – it works wonderfully…

My heart is currently broken in two. One half resides in South Africa where my old roots still remain, and my heart still longs for the endless beaches and the smell of moist soil after a summer downpour. My love for Ma Afrika will never fade. The other half of me has been transplanted to the Land of the Long White Cloud. The land of the Taniwha, beautiful Maraes, and volcanoes. The land of green, pure beauty that truly inspires. And because I am so torn between these two lands – I shall forever remain cross-eyed.

Stalk Tee here:
www.tgayer.com
tee@tgayer.com

facebook.com/TGAyerAuthor

twitter.com/TGAyerAuthor

bookbub.com/profile/t-g-ayer

9 780473 429249